FINAL TRUTH

by

John Behardien

Duncurin
Publishing

Duncurin.com

First Published in England MMXVII

Duncurin Publishing
Monton
England

Duncurin.com

ISBN : 978-0-9935169-6-2

Book Design : Sheepie

DEDICATION

For Sue, Colin and Annie, Mark and Liz and Glenys.
With love.

WITH THANKS

My sincere thanks to the following very talented people.

Patrick Fahy: for his painstaking Copy/Edit skills, patfahy@lineone.net

Paul Gurney: For cover design, paul@thegraphicdesignworkshop.co.uk

Cover Photo: Courtesy of PicturesofVancouver.com

Other Books By John Behardien

Crack In the Code
Stars' End

The Last Great Gift

Dawn Over Vancouver
All That Time Allows (for release 2018)

Final Horizon
Final Request
Final Truth

One Life Many Moments

CONTENTS

CHAPTER 1

Run Forever

The pavement remained a little moist after the recent rain that had gone over not an hour before. This, however, was not the reason for the uncertain, faltering walk. Her feelings of fear and panic mounted with every step she took. Moreover, as she noticed their clammy sheen, it was almost as if the concrete flags were weeping inside, just as she was. Each mark, crack and blemish was still so familiar for she'd looked down, as she did now, on countless occasions, not daring to lift her head. The times she'd traversed this exact route when she'd approached with nothing less than abject terror that permeated down to her naked soul – feelings she still recognised as if it were yesterday. Nor could she forget the episodes when she'd run in the opposite direction and hidden; knowing only that she'd have to return, lest the worse fate that she'd been threatened with should overtake her.

There was the Williams' house. She remembered the kindly elderly couple who'd found her, more than once, sheltering beneath the rhododendron bush in their front garden, sobbing for a life that was lost and the misery that had replaced it. She thought the darkness under its waxy leaves would protect her, insulate her from her torment: but this, sadly, was the thing about the dark, it held only more horror. They'd been unfailingly kind, asking her indoors, into the light, for milk and a chocolate biscuit, or two. Mr Williams would look expectantly as he held the biscuit tin for her inspection; his bushy greyed eyebrows framed similar grey eyes, which retained a spark and a delight that matched his

1

fatherly smile. Mrs Williams with the gnarled knuckles but smooth soft skin would hold her hand, rub her frozen palms and put a reassuring arm on her shoulders. Even as she'd stopped shaking, they'd phone the man, who was rather more of a monster than a man, to come and collect her. He'd appear quickly on such occasions, almost as if he were frightened as to what she would reveal to the nice, childless couple. Her sad and sunken eyes would make manifest her recurring wish: if only she'd gone to live with them, she was sure she could have had some peace and live a calm but desolate life, quietly missing her loved ones but at least without the abuse that had befallen her.

She used to feel the sickness, she recognised now, at the very sight of him. His weak, jutting jaw which was covered by his rancid beard. The eyes that seemed too large and too close together to be accommodated by even a man's face and the insincere looks that they gave out at every turn. Furthermore, there was the all-pervading smell of burnt chip fat that seemed to fill the room as soon as he stepped inside. He'd shrug his shoulders knowingly at the elderly couple. He'd assure them that the retching that overran her was surely due to her gulping her milk too quickly. He'd then test them with a typical shifty look while he wondered if they would accept the scenario he'd hastily assembled. Being emboldened by their gentle nods he'd then suggest that it was perhaps only to be expected; that surely losing one's parents was so traumatic that she'd need more time. He'd agree with them quickly; yes, this was the reason why she'd lost so much weight. Without doubt, it was a good job that social services had placed her with him, so that he could make sure she was looked after. All the couple had to do was to let him know and he'd come round straight away to collect her.

Then, as their suspicions were becalmed on plausible posturing, so much easier to contemplate than the truth, he would feign concern and fatherly affection that was as false as the front he'd constructed so as to allow him to continue to abuse her. There were, no doubt, countless other girls that had come within his depraved circle, right under the noses of social services, who knew only that they could rely on him to take in troubled young girls at a moment's notice and with no questions asked. That was the problem – no questions were ever asked.

He'd walk back up the road with her, the way she was moving now. He'd place an affectionate palm on her shoulder that would rub her gently until the Williams had waved and closed their front door. At such time the grip became much firmer, bordering on pain, and more insistent as he'd remind her that if she tried to run, he would find her. Having done so he would have her committed at the age of thirteen to an orphanage where a pretty thing like her would be passed round by *really* wicked people continually and repeatedly until they'd all had their fill of her slim form and young body. 'What they'd do to her would be horrible and very unlike the simple warmth and comfort he asked of her.' She wondered as time passed if there could possibly be more evil people than him. For sure, such nights, the ones in which she'd dared to even think of escape, would be his most violent where he'd find new ways to abuse and new obscene acts with which to torment her, an innocent child. Pain, in all its forms, was the electricity that ran through his body and at every verse end he would be generous and unceasing with its usage.

She stopped. She was nearly at the house. She recognised the old gate still hanging off its hinges but in a more advanced state of decay than the day she'd walked away, never to return, at least, until today. The house seemed smaller than she remembered; perhaps she'd become used to more spacious homes; perhaps she'd simply exaggerated the size of the prison where such dreadful things had been visited upon her. She started shaking; her hand came up to her face as she dipped her eyes behind her palm. "I can't do it. I can't go back." She swallowed vigorously to the point of gasping but nonetheless felt she was choking. She was drowning in dry air. "Please don't make me," she beseeched. Her forehead now began to perspire and the shaking seemed to intensify in perfect unison with her voice that broke up while her throat became as dry sand in an arid desert.

Toby stopped and held her hand. His own hand was uncharacteristically sweaty as he masterfully tried to conceal its trembling from her. "You don't have to do this, Clancy. I told you *we* can handle it. You don't have to face him; you can simply get back in the car. We will get all the information we require." For the first time in his life, his lie was almost undiscoverable. In point of fact she nearly allowed herself to believe it. How she desperately wanted to accept this at face value and turn with him and get back into the leathery and cossetted refuge of the Bentley. Surely others could face and denounce her abuser. Crucially, it was the depth of immaculate concern that he showed that helped her to continue. Furthermore, it was his worthy, but flawed, attempt to protect her that was the only thing that allowed brave words to appear, before she ran forever from the dreadful scene.

"No, Toby, we have to finish this. *I* have to do this, to end it *today*, once and for all," her voice now cracking like an ancient gramophone. She hastily wiped away her tears. Tears that were as much to do with her fear as the anger she felt over her stolen childhood. She pulled herself up to her full height, then came the slow deep breath followed by the gentle exhalation. She was ready.

She extended her right palm to appear in front of him, but didn't look at him. She walked on, now alone, ready for the first time in fifteen years to face the man whose summary execution would be a kindness: a kindness that she did not feel like bestowing. She retained a far worse fate for him uppermost in her mind; if only she could hold it together for long enough. The sense of loss Toby felt, as he let her go forwards on her own, was only barely eclipsed by the memory of the day he buried his parents and his little sister, a month before she'd come to live with him.

The precise, rhythmical clip that usually came from her heels as she walked was replaced by something much more erratic: erratic but at least moving forwards. Ultimately, it was her anger as well as her outrage that now fuelled her progress, together with the final thought – that without her coming through this, then she would never know peace. Above all, she craved this more than anything else. Although she recognised that nothing would now fill the void that had opened within, she would at least have that. As was the way with such things an even more brutal thought entered her overwrought mind. If she did not take action, then how many other girls would be further abused by this monster? And the cruellest thought indeed, how many girls had been harmed because of her inaction through all these years?

It came to her in that moment. In those closing seconds she remembered the strategy that she'd adopted on those interminable nights when he'd done such horrible things to her. She would detach herself, somehow, from her own body; almost standing apart from it as those cruel deeds were carried out on a lifeless shell that had no sensation, no feeling and surely no soul; by distancing herself in this way as might a spectator in a cinema bearing witness to abominable acts on screen but from an insulating distance. She relied on this now and it was almost as if she were walking with, but was totally detached from, that young woman who'd, by some means, found the strength to continue her steps.

She tapped on the door, its rotten frame and peeling paint clearly not touched since the day fifteen years ago, the day she left. Rubbish was overflowing from wheelie bins that he'd not bothered to drag the few yards down his driveway. He came to the door, recognising her immediately. He looked behind into the house almost nervously and then walked forwards, stepping outside.

"Penny, well fancy seeing you."

He closed the door furtively behind him and came out onto the broken and weed-strewn drive. "Rachel is sleeping," he offered.

Clancy had always wondered how much she knew, how much had been hidden from her and how much she'd guessed. For sure, he was an inveterate liar, showman and at all times seemed nothing but plausible – until the lights went out. At such time, she'd hear the creaking boards and the living nightmares would begin. How could his wife not have known? In the event she would know soon enough. Clancy was now certain that it would be today.

"Still not working, eh Roy? That bad back and, oh what was it now? Nervous exhaustion, troubling you as always?"

"I've told you, Penny, what's the point in workin' when bein' on the sick pays me so genrussly not to bother!"

She laughed as she looked round at the dilapidated front of the house. He laughed in unison, his bearing one of triumph rather than shame.

Her smile evaporated like propellant discharging in a shell casing. "I'm here for you Roy." Her head, in that moment, began nodding firmly with the certainty of her actions. "It's time for you to face your accusers, own up to your misdemeanours." Her voice, somehow, finding a clear but deeper register than she'd found it to be capable of: like a judge passing sentence.

"And would *you* be one of those, eh, Penny? Seems to me nobody would believe a troubled girl like you fifteen years ago and they won't believe you *now*." He looked her up and down, pausing over her chest and legs while proprietorial eyes flared. "*My*, we do scrub up nice. You look wonderful. Have you time for a quick one while Rachel's asleep?"

Clancy's flesh crawled under his lascivious gaze; she could have sworn that he licked his lips.

"I don't think you'll be saying that very soon, Roy."

He feigned fear on his face as his lips cooed together mockingly. "Ah, are you gonna work me over? Beat me up eh, go on take a swing, one for old times. Take me down to Littleton nick, p'rhaps, force a *confesshun*. Like that's gonna happun, *duh*. You couldn't tell them *then* and what'ya gonna tellum *now*?" He laughed mockingly with deceitful concern, as only an abuser who faced the abused could and, once again, he revelled in the power and the pain. Dark, glassy eyes flared with the narcotic of sheer torment as they bore into her.

"I just wonder how many of those girls, that you were supposed to protect, were abused by you."

"And they, like you, luvved ev'ry minute."

"I was thirteen, still a child."

"Oh no, not a child. I can remembuh very well, your body was not a child's. In any case you soon became a woman under my inflooence."

Her body shook with revulsion, compounded by his resurgent, smug self-satisfaction.

"You go on telling yourself that, Roy. Tell the folks who will find you and tap you on the shoulder in prison that, too. You are nothing but a sadistic paedophile abuser who took in vulnerable kids like me and then used them to satisfy your sexual depravity. You destroyed a grieving girl's childhood in order to inflict your debauched sexual cravings. You are a monster in every form of that word."

"And who cares! Do you think social services cared about *you*? They just wanted to wash their hands of kids like you and I was simply willing to take them all like so much unwanted *rubbish*."

"And you repaid them with destroying, no doubt, countless young girls' lives, as well as mine."

"They loved *every* minute, just like you. Besides, it doesn't seem to have worked out badly for you." Once again, he cast dark eyes over her. "An expensive dress, classy shoes and that luvvely watch on your wrist, which looks real. Just *who* are you satisfyin' now, eh Penny? Are you sure you don't want a quick one? We could take up where we left off."

"No, I am going to make sure you go away for a very long time. What they will do to you in prison will more than settle scores: a nice taste of your own medicine."

He laughed again, one that became so deep that he had to tilt his chest back to give proper voice to it.

"And I've told you *nobody* will believe yuh." He placed emphasis on that absolute as if he was trying to explain a given fact to an impotent child. "You are wastin' your breath. Who are yuh gonna tell? I will just deny everything. Don't come here and threaten me. Do you think anyone will believe you and what proof do you have? So I slept with a few young girls – I was only taking what I was owed to me in housing *scum* like you. I was only taking a bit of kindness from those who didn't know anything else and those who didn't care. I deserved payment in kind for havin' unwanted *nothings*, like you, in my house."

She interrupted his proselytising, "And boy did you exact that, Roy. Just why was that, Roy? I think I know; I worked it all out. Rachel didn't give you much, did she Roy? That's when you took it out on me. Night after night all those execrable acts visited on me and, no doubt, many others. All those things you wanted to do to her and couldn't." He reacted so quickly that she knew she'd found the key to bring him down.

"Don't come here with your fancy words, you're nothin' but a commun bitch. I'd *never* do that to her, you leave her out of it."

It was Clancy's turn to laugh. "Oh so precious Rachel, but defiling the bodies of a few innocent kids is okay! That's it isn't it, Roy? Dear Rachel is *frigid*, gave you *nothing*, so you took it all out on children. Innocent children."

"You leave my Rachel out of this, you no good whore!" His eyes bled hatred and outrage as he glared at her, whilst spitting the words into her face.

She held on, masterfully resisting the urge to destroy that evil face, now an object of detestation and no longer one of fear: she was almost through. She half hoped that he would try to hit her, then for certain she'd have more than enough excuse to carry out the acts that her honed form longed to entrain and beat him until he lay unconscious at her feet. Surely the minimum he deserved. She realised, however, that once started, she wouldn't be able to stop until that face was a bloodied mess and he would escape what she had planned for him. She accepted that others would have to judge him, and be seen to have done so, in order for his punishment to have meaning.

"Or what Roy, you'll rape me all over again?" His expression changed to the one that she now realised had been on his face night after night when he came to her in the dark. He approached with more menace, about to undo his belt. "Rapin' you is the least I'm gonna do to you. Reckon you're overdue another session from me. I'll start where I left off. Fuckin' you's the least I'll do and who'll care about a little orphan girl, scrubbed up or otherwise. Come 'ere, you won't be able to sit down for a week after I've finished with yuh."

In purely a reflex move her left arm extended and a long slim finger pointed accusingly at him. "Well, they care now Roy." Suddenly, she turned away and touched the lapel on her raincoat.

"Have we got enough?"

All at once, he realised that her conversation was with someone else: someone who'd been there the entire time. The tiny earpiece, disguised as an earring, hissed into life.

"Have we! Clancy, we have got more than enough on this scum bag," returned Toby's voice with glee.

Roy lunged forward and tried to grab Clancy by the throat. She sidestepped quickly and pushed him with a casual open palm as he missed her. He fell awkwardly on to the overrun garden. He looked up glaring at her. She was taller than he'd ever remembered. Correspondingly, he was reduced to a figure of pity – almost.

"Oh, Roy, you are not worth my getting my hands dirty. Goodbye, Roy. I suspect things will change quickly for you from this point on. I have a feeling it's payback time. I reckon you have about fifteen seconds of freedom – not even enough time to confess to Rachel." A murderous look appeared on his face, but only for a moment. His fear, no longer feigned, rose with the sweat precipitating round his neck, like a noose. Having begun, it extended its influence upon a guilty party, as only it can, when called to account. He went in those seconds from being her abuser, someone who was always in control to someone who was about to lose everything as the tables turned finally but so irrevocably.

She turned and walked down the overgrown pathway full of weeds. Her walk was now far more certain. She didn't look back. It was over. Her only regret, which overbalanced any satisfaction, that she hadn't done it sooner. Police officers passed her as she did so. Waiting for her on the pavement was Toby just as he had all those years ago.

She fell into his arms. Toby held her firmly. He realised that he was, in that moment, the only thing keeping her upright as she wept repeatedly. He brushed the lustrous brown hair, soft like spun sugar, that gave off that delightful smell as he did so. For a minute or two neither moved apart from the convulsive sobs that wracked her body as she reverted to the young teenager who'd arrived to live with him all alone, without a soul in the world. He whispered; his own eyes now overrun with tears that he could not stop. "Well done, Penny. I've seen you do so many brave things but none so brave as this today."

Time stopped for as long as it took for both of them to, barely, compose themselves. After a while they walked to the Bentley; he held the door open, still gripping her hand. His driver had been frozen to his seat, unable to get out of the car. Alexis was sitting in the other rear seat. She hugged Clancy, as soon as she got in, but neither woman could, for the moment, speak. Alexis coughed in an attempt to clear her throat and also to quench some of the tears that burned within.

After a while Clancy asked "Are you sure we got enough?" Her voice faltered with nervousness.

"More than sure, Clancy, the Police will be all over the house seizing his computer and, with the testimony from others, he will go away for a very long time, I promise. He will not evade me or the team I have assembled, who will make sure that the punishment fits his crimes. We'll certainly push for him to be in prison for a long time. As you know, paedophile abusers don't do too well once inside. Once we have the Social Services files and have interviewed all his previous protected kids we will be able to demonstrate the enormity of his crimes and what a danger to young vulnerable girls he remains. It's over Clancy. This is my promise."

Toby, having done his best to compose himself, closed the rear door and then occupied the front passenger seat. The door shut with a secure 'thunk' as if it were underlining the closing of a chapter. Alexis looked ashen still desperately trying, but ultimately failing, to stop the tears from precipitating in her own eyes.

Clancy managed a glance in his direction. His eyes remained at their deepest most grave shade of blue. Toby never broke a promise. He'd not done so in fifteen years; she knew he wouldn't start now. Clancy nodded but another thought came to her in that moment as ideas that had been forming for some time crystallised finally within. Having done so, she knew that those ideas would not depart. This was to be her final act. It really was over.

CHAPTER II

Single Hint

For the moment all four sat there as if frozen in time and completely unable to move. Clancy looked away, as silence fell among them, choosing the refuge of the window rather than attempt to fill that void. The driver gripped the steering wheel frustratedly but redundantly. He could only think to himself that it was a good job that the police were on the scene, as he would dearly have loved to take the substantial car jack from his boot to 'that bastard' whose treatment of Clancy was unconscionable. He had neither seen her look so dreadful nor so vulnerable – not even on the day that they'd collected her.

Clancy stared through the tinted car window, trusting neither her expression nor any words in that moment. She gave off a long sigh like steam escaping from a leaking pipe, suddenly feeling older than her 28 years. As Toby looked behind from the front seat he and Alexis glanced at each other. She dabbed frantically at the tears knowing that engaging with Clancy was more important than her own feelings. The couple were desperate to find words of comfort for the distraught woman and yet silence was the only thing that plumbed the depths of her despair.

Not for the first time, Toby sought to clarify things by repetition. "It's over Penny, it's finished. We have all we need. He'll go away for a long, long time and will never prey on young girls again." Clancy looked briefly at him as his words slowed to a stop, then retrained her gaze through the safety of the window and on to the familiar street. She couldn't help but notice the promise of a new spring to finally banish the long winter: a winter where she'd forfeited everything. Another most grievous loss was the one that she'd waited 28 years for, one that might have shone in the dark of her loneliness, only to have such a thing plucked away from her just at the point of realisation that this is what she'd craved all this time.

Toby indicated to the driver to get underway. The W12 power plant caught immediately with a brief shimmer of the long, highly-polished bonnet but otherwise gave no clue that the engine was running. The accelerator was called upon and the car began to move away from the scene associated with such dreadful memories.

A silence known only to planetary bodies in the vastness of space descended again; Alexis knew that she could bear it no longer. Inevitably, searching for words to comfort the female agent, she chose the wrong ones. "Have you heard from Tim?"

Clancy, upon registering the question, turned from the window. Toby could see that she remained on the edge of tears that once begun would not stop. Sensing, however, that neither of them were in receipt of the full events of that day her expression brightened, just a little, banishing the tears as it did so.

"You don't know do you, either of you, what happened that last day?" The driver spent so long looking in the mirror that the collision avoidance system had to apply the brakes automatically as a double-decker bus loomed hard in front of the Bentley.

"No, in truth, I don't," interrupted Toby. His eyes were now aflame with curiosity, unmasking questions that he'd hitherto dared not ask. The slight hum from the engine and subdued tyre noise were the only sounds that broke the otherwise deep silence. Eventually, the pause ended and, like a storyteller opening the first page of a new, but heart-breaking, book, she began, "Toby, I think you'd just arrived as they took him away in the ambulance."

The briefest of smiles appeared on Clancy's face but before it expired it left behind just the slightest hint of intrigue as she was about to convey information that the three others in the car were strangers to.

"It was a few days before Christmas, as you know. There we were at the side of the road; myself sister Munro, the paramedic and Mr Charles, the surgeon. The ambulance crew had arrived and parked in front of the taxi that they then pushed away so that they could reverse to come closer to their patient. Tim had flatlined. Sister Munro said he'd 'gone' and that it was hopeless. I'd shouted at the film crew that this was not news but it was a cruel intrusion upon a poor man who should be allowed to die in peace. The paramedics had blocked the road and were about to erect screens to shield Tim's body so that we could get him in the back of the ambulance and take him to the mortuary. Just at that moment, Janet was passing on her bike, travelling to work."

"Is Janet the one who worked at the coffee shop?" asked Alexis. "Is that what she was, *a barista*?" she clarified, her large blue eyes seemingly even larger than usual.

"Yes, that's just about it," Clancy confirmed, as the merest hint of a glimmer appeared in her eyes, reflecting the other woman's incredulous wonderment. She continued, "Janet saw Tim or, I should say, Tim's *body* on the floor. His blood was all over the pavement. They'd used all the supplies they had in transfusing him. She jumped off her bike leaving it in the middle of the road and rushed towards Mr Charles. As she brandished two bare arms, she spoke these words, looking him straight in the eye.

'I'm 'O' negative. You can use that, *right*? It's universal donor blood, *right*?'

The surgeon then said that it was too late Tim had slipped away.

She screamed at him, holding up her arms, 'Take it, take it *all*. Take it *now*, but don't let him *die*. Save him; do it and do it now!'

Mr Charles told her calmly that Tim had arrested; the position was hopeless. Even then she wouldn't have it.

'Can't you shock him or something, what about CPR? Do something, do *anything*, but don't let him die, not today, not like this and not on this sidewalk. Man up fucker!'

She then lay on the pavement next to Tim held her arms up and shouted, 'Now, use my blood, use it all but save him! Now!' I think he was really taken aback, I doubt anyone had spoken to him like that before!" Clancy paused in remembering and also to allow them to take in what she'd said. She then continued.

"All I could do was to stand back and watch. They started CPR; they set up a drip from her arm to Tim's. In a flurry of activity, Mr Charles shocked him with the defibrillator, then gave him an injection of adrenaline straight into his heart and shocked him again. She kept telling them to take all her blood; that they were not to stop until she had none left. Then a motorcycle arrived with a further ten units of 'O' negative blood, like Janet's.

Suddenly, Mr Charles stood up with triumph on his face. He announced that he'd got it."

"Got what?" asked Alexis, her eyes even wider than when Clancy had begun.

"He'd clamped the spurting artery that was causing Tim's haemorrhage. They then packed Tim into the ambulance. Mr Charles announced from the rear step of the ambulance, like a declaration of defiance, that he was going to be okay. Janet insisted on jumping in with the patient and they sped away bound for Hope Hospital. I was left standing on the pavement, which is when you came Toby."

"Have you seen him, Penny?" asked Alexis cautiously, sensing that there was more to learn.

"Yes, I saw him briefly on critical care. Janet had not left his side."

"And since then? So, Tim's okay?" Alexis needed to clarify.

"Yes, he's recovering nicely," Toby confirmed.

Not quite seeing the full picture and being aware of the strained glances between Clancy and Toby, Alexis knew that something else had happened, something she'd not picked up.

She then asked, "So, that's okay then, isn't it?"

Knowing a little more than Alexis and seeing the angst building on his colleague's face Toby asked, "How much does Tim remember?"

This was it; the crux of the matter. Alexis saw it all come into focus with this one question.

She anticipated Clancy's answer even before she uttered the words.

"Nothing, he remembers *absolutely nothing* at all. He remembers falling after he was shot and then waking up in critical care. I suppose it's best that way," she offered after a slight pause allowing another tear to form in her sore eyes.

"Have you had time to talk?"

"No not really, Janet has been with him his entire convalescence. Even since starting her training."

"She's started her training already!"

Alexis now looked sharply at Toby, as if he'd committed treason. He struggled to make his expression as neutral as possible, which only served to make him appear guiltier. He certainly couldn't admit that she'd almost completed the programme.

Cautiously he said, shrugging his shoulders, "What could I say? She just said that whatever we were up to she wanted to be in on it and she wasn't going to let him out of her sight. And she hasn't." Acute distress formed on Alexis' face but not on Clancy's, as if the latter were already resigned to the fate that Alexis had only now worked out.

"So, let me just get this right. Janet comes up to you and says she wants to get involved and become an agent. I have nothing against coffee shop girls but surely what have you been screening people for all of these years, only inviting the best after careful scrutiny, if just anyone can bang on your door and say, 'Giss a job Mistoh!'."

Out of the corner of his eye he saw a slight flicker of a smile forming on Clancy's face. His inability to respond to this only increased his own awkwardness. She was, however, still unable to meet his desperate need for another to make eye contact rather than the steely gaze that Alexis had set upon him. Toby now became very defensive; furthermore, his driver was doing his best to stifle a fit of the giggles and gave off a loud cough that resonated through the plush and refined interior.

"Well, Alexis, it wasn't *quite* like that."

"Okay then, how was it? Can I bang on your door and become an agent?"

"No! No, I mean yes, if you wish!"

"That's not what you said when I saved your *hide* from under that avalanche."

"Yes, I admit it I did say you were too precious to risk in this way, but don't think for a heartbeat that it was because I thought you didn't have the ability."

"And Janet? I take it she does?"

"Alexis," he said, with just a hint of pleading mixing with his discomfiture, "she told me that she'd saved Tim; put herself on the line for him. She then said that surely this counted for something and she should be given a chance to do what we did."

"And *who* told her about what you did?"

"Certainly not any of us. I think she just reasoned that his getting shot in this way and Clancy's getting over there to take out the Russian guy could only mean that we weren't doing *pottery*."

Alexis' expression finally softened into a smile; she was ready to release him from her close scrutiny – almost. "So, you *caved in* and said you'd sign her up?"

"No, Alexis! I said that I'd give her a *trial*, see what she could do and if she passed the assessment that we put her through, then we'd train her."

"And?"

"Well, it has to be said that she came through. She performed better than some of our more experienced agents and what she didn't know she soon learned." Finally, Toby's frustration boiled over. "Look, Alexis, what's all this about? So, we gave her a chance and she came through, I couldn't then turn her down. Why have you set against her so?"

Toby had missed the real reason behind Alexis' unease with regard to their new recruit. His only clue, if he'd been perceptive enough to access it, was the solicitous look she darted in Clancy's direction. Unfortunately, he'd missed this single hint she gave out, his perceptive streak being subsumed by her interlocution and the defensive stance he'd had to adopt.

Silence once again descended in the car. Each was embroiled with their private thoughts. Alexis in particular struggled to process all the new information she'd been given and realised that she could neither voice concern for Clancy nor reveal that she now knew what was weighing upon her even more than the traumas that she'd recently come through.

In the event, before Alexis could resolve what seemed insoluble, the Bentley approached the security gate leading to Clancy's apartment. The car stopped, giving off a slight hissing noise from the climate control as it pulsated smoothly on the hard standing that lay in front of the grounds poised to fully embrace spring. Clancy got out of the car and Toby jumped out, too.

He saw her take a deep breath but otherwise had no inkling as to what she was about to reveal. "I'm finished, Toby."

He had been totally wrong-footed by the conversation in the car; even then he did not grasp what she was telling him. He wondered later if the enormity of what she'd really said had prevented him from registering it.

"Yes, Clancy, it's all finished. We can get back to normal, there's a lot to be done."

"No, Toby, *I'm* finished, I quit. I realise I can't do this any more." A pause like a gulf separating continents formed; his mouth opened a couple of times but it was only at his third attempt that he was able to breach it.

"Look, Clancy, you are tired; let's have a week or two on the *Ma Puissance* and see how you feel then?" His voice, once again, took on pleading tones, but now for a very different reason as he detected the resolve behind her words.

"No, Toby, a holiday will not change the way I feel. Not tomorrow, not next week nor next month."

He paused as the reality hit him with its finality. "You are serious aren't you?" His head shook with the words, as if they were counting down his own execution.

"Very much so," she replied, nodding slowly but decisively.

"I can't do this without you, Clancy, I couldn't and wouldn't. You have been with me forever; I would not want to go forward without you." His face distorted with a degree of pain that she'd not seen since the day that she'd overturned the china cabinet. So much so that she knew that she had to attempt to rescue him from its depths.

She smiled and touched his shoulder. "You say that, and I believe you. You are busier than ever, with so many vital missions in front of you. I *know* you'll be fine, just as I know it's time for me to leave. Tim has really come on. Now he's recovered he will just get better and better. He and Janet are very good together; I think they'll be a very effective team." She surveyed him carefully, hoping that he would be able to accept at least some of her conclusions.

"My mind's made up, Toby, goodbye." With this she kissed him, and with no more words being spoken she activated the security gate and walked into the entrance without glancing back.

Numbness and incredulity submerged him under a shockwave of despair. He thought he was going to be sick. As he held the rear door open he could barely summon his dry cracked voice to inform Alexis, "Clancy's resigned." She looked at him, his features pale and wan, but not for the first time that day lost for words. Alexis saw Clancy's figure departing as she walked away, the nightmare that she'd dared to contemplate had become manifest. She wondered how Toby could possibly cope without her.

His driver darted a sharp look in the rear-view mirror and could not help but stare at the door that Clancy had walked through. Toby practically stumbled into the rear seat while his driver wondered if they'd ever see her again and if any of them could possibly get over the sense of loss he, and no doubt they, felt. He could understand why Toby looked as pallid as he did; he had surely been visited by a ghost that having appeared would never depart. His stomach churned uneasily as it mirrored his boss' expression.

Alexis looked steadily at him. "You don't see it, do you?"

"What?"

She slowed down her speech as if to reflect her own concern and the need to explain something momentous to someone who'd seen nothing. "She's in love."

She thought to herself that if he asked with whom she would have to physically shake him. Instead he committed an even greater sin, "What, Clancy? In love?" Alexis glanced at his shin and had he not looked so dreadful she would have aimed a sharp kick at its bony vulnerability. Mercifully for all those present, after a slight pause, he registered what Alexis had known for some considerable time.

"Tim?"

"Tim!"

"Forgive me, Alexis. I realise what you've been trying to tell me and why you are upset about Janet."

"Toby, you are the most wonderful man I have ever known, but sometimes, just sometimes…"

"Yes, yes I know I can be stupid?"

"Not quite what I was going to say but close enough."

"Well, I can see now. Is there anything I can do?"

"I suspect not, I'm thinking that your new recruit, the ex-coffee shop girl, is firmly in charge of the situation and Penny can see this more clearly than I can."

The Bentley made slow, almost funereal, progress away from Clancy's apartment. It was as though none of the occupants wanted to leave. Toby tried phoning later the same day. He eventually left a voicemail to say that his solicitors had more than enough to go on and that the Crown Prosecution Service had agreed to take the case. The next day he tried calling round. He peered through into the secure garage to see if he could see Clancy's white F-Type. Failing on all fronts, he then left a note, slipping it under her door, after pleading with a neighbour to be let in.

Some weeks went by and despite making repeated attempts, Toby failed on each and every occasion to contact Clancy. Alexis, too, tried to contact her, as did many of the agents. Eventually they realised two things. One was that Clancy was serious about leaving and the second that, when someone with her experience didn't want to be found, then it was unlikely that they'd succeed.

CHAPTER III

Panic Button

One day in late spring, Mrs Wainwright had gone into the kitchen to get some drinks for herself and Arthur, who was sitting admiring his lawn as he sat in the garden. She noticed a gleaming white sports car appear in the CCTV camera mounted on their gate. Although she didn't recognise the vehicle, she knew immediately who was behind the wheel even without that person either lowering a window to speak into the intercom, or vacating the car. Immediately, she pressed the release button and the significant weight of metal began to swing with its usual smooth and noiseless efficiency.

She called through the house excitedly to her husband. Once again, and as a rerun of the first time they'd met, both she and Arthur waited excitedly for Clancy to get out of the white F-Type. Margaret went down the stone steps as soon as the door opened in order to hug her. Arthur, for once, looked at the young woman's face and not at her legs as he expressed fatherly concern.

"Penny, it's so nice to see you. You've made our day! You look so well," said the older woman lying and "So do you, Margaret," came from the younger one with more truth.

"Come in, come in. It's been such a lovely day. We were sitting in the garden; I just popped into the kitchen when I saw your car approach the gates."

Margaret led their guest through the kitchen. Clancy nodded to Mariah their maid as they passed into the back garden.

"Sit down, Penny, Arthur will go and find another seat. *Quickly*, Arthur, before Mariah starts fussing over us. I'll just get some tea and some cold drinks while you sit down. And Arthur, I think we've earned some *cake* now that we have a guest?" she added with more finality than doubt.

He glanced at his tummy and his tight waistband but nodded his acquiescence, nevertheless, just as he always did when faced with a determined pronouncement from his wife. Margaret returned a few minutes later and saw that Arthur had found another chair and was discussing, with their guest, the recent planting, overseen by him, but carried out by their gardener, in the grounds. His left hand swept creatively over the large estate that lay before them. Mrs Wainwright, however, had much more important things to discuss. As was her wont, as soon as she'd sat down and poured the drinks, her pale-blue eyes were levelled inquisitively in Clancy's direction.

"Tim tells me you've resigned?"

"Yes, Margaret, that's correct."

"I never thought I'd hear such a thing."

"No, Margaret, and I never thought I'd say such a thing." Clancy looked away briefly from the keen gaze as she sensed the gushing questions behind it.

"I bet so many are missing you, especially Toby. Tim says he'll be lost without you. That they'll *all* be lost without you."

"People move on, Margaret, I felt it was time for me to do the same," she offered as she squinted conveniently into the oblique but intense sunshine.

Margaret nodded; however, this served only for her to formulate more of the questions ranged on her 'urgent' list.

"May I ask," Clancy smiled as she heard the words, usually coming from Tim, "any special reason?"

"Well, one or two things are settled. One or two people have moved on. Now is a good time."

"But what will you do? A young woman like you?"

"Well, Margaret, that's why I am here today. I'm leaving."

The older woman looked even more perturbed. She coughed nervously, as if she was trying to expel something unpalatable, but in truth she'd already anticipated the reason for Clancy's visit.

"*Leaving*? Where will you go?"

"I'm not quite sure yet. I thought a little travelling; they say it broadens the mind."

Margaret laughed.

"Not that I had you down for a little cottage in Cornwall, but I would have thought you've already done more travelling than most."

The lovely smile, that she knew her son had fallen in love with at its first outing, was displayed all too briefly in her direction.

"I'm thinking that there is always room for a little more, Margaret; it's a big world."

"Yes," the older woman formed her reply to Clancy but she was already looking in the direction of her husband. "Arthur, *Dear*, time for more drinks?" He looked at the tray of drinks, barely touched. "A nice cup of tea: I'm sure Penny would *love* another cup. And cake, bring some more cake."

He then looked at their guest's cup; more than half full, but had not yet latched on to his wife's thoughts. "But *Mariah* will get them when we are ready?"

"*No*, Arthur, I'd like *you* to do that, please. *Now*, would be good." The pale eyes instantly took on the appearance of chiselled ice. Arthur moved without further hesitation, finally realising that his wife wanted Clancy to herself. As soon as he'd vacated his chair, the eyes rotated to focus on Clancy, who smiled as the older lady's expression softened when applied in her direction. She waited only for so long as to allow her husband to vacate the perimeter to which her subdued voice might extend.

"He *loves* you, Penny." A pause followed as the words hung in the ether of the crisp dry day. Still, the steady gaze was held in Clancy's direction and was only broken by an intense shaft of sunshine as it emerged from an obscuring dense cloud.

She continued, "I can see that. I also know the moment it happened. It must have been the very day he looked up at you from that sordid, crooked card table – the night *you* saved him."

Slowly and carefully, her voice dry and faltering uncomfortably, Penny inserted, "I think, Margaret, that someone else has saved him now."

"I suspect that's because he doesn't know what's *really* happened; only what he's been told. Only *you* can tell him what's happened, Penny. Why not *do* that?"

"Surely, Margaret, that's trapped in the past now. He believes what he believes."

A little twinkle of incredulity appeared as an overlay in the limitless cerulean of her eyes that shamed a perfect sky; ones that had neither blinked nor strayed as much as a millimetre from the pretty face with the eyes of a deep brown like Cuban mahogany.

She spoke eagerly. "You know, Penny, I've seen Tim with a lot of girls, back when he was squandering his life. No offence, but they'd turn up, they'd giggle a bit, spend the night and, to be fair, in the morning they'd still be giggling. Then, they'd leave and we wouldn't see them again, and neither would he. I'd wonder if they were wasting their lives or perhaps how much there could possibly *be* in their lives – as, clearly, there wasn't much in his. For sure, he was just drifting through his youth. Things went up a gear, but not in a good way, when he took up residence in our apartment in Mougins. Although we didn't see him, he continued to act with gay abandon and, no doubt, never formed anything approaching a *meaningful* relationship. We were so worried about him. That's when Arthur contacted Horizon. Then, one day, you came. You snapped your fingers and dragged him out of that *dreadful* place and out of that life. And, yes, I know it nearly killed him, but in truth before he joined you in Horizon he wasn't alive anyway. Not only did you save him, but I believe you showed him something still more important..."

A further delay opened as Margaret chose her words with care. The younger woman nodded for her to continue but otherwise didn't form speech. Margaret then obliged, "I think you showed him, for the first time ever in his wasted existence, a sense of *purpose*. It's almost as though his life had just begun; an awakening, if you like. Although he's been distracted, I think this is a temporary thing."

"Margaret, I think that Janet is much more than a distraction. Or, perhaps I should say she's neither a distraction nor temporary."

"Ooh, I'm not too sure about that. You see, Penny, the crux of the matter," she then paused again just to allow the smile with a slightest hint of triumph to form. She began again, now turning her head slightly obliquely but thereby allowing her closer eye to form a knowing wink as she nevertheless continued to gaze at and tantalise the female agent. "The *heart* of it, not that even he knows it – yet – is that you've also shown him things to be worthy of; *people* to be worthy of. This is all new to him, as I believe you realise. Now, once he's *seen that*, all else will sooner or later pale by comparison."

"Don't you think Janet is providing all that he requires?"

"Well, Penny, no offence but I am not at all keen on that young woman. I'm not a snob, people don't have to have *breeding* or anything like that, but I do know that whatever they need – she's *not* got. She is brash and she's coarse and sooner or later he *will* see that. Besides, Penny, we are forgetting one tiny thing. I know and *he* knows that he loves you! What's more, and forgive my directness, but I suspect that you know that too. What he needs is really very simple, a *normal* loving relationship. I am of the view that you've never turned your back on a challenge; *surely*, this is not the time to start, is it?"

Clancy smiled but simply continued to gaze at the perceptive older woman. Only then did Margaret glance away as she prepared the most difficult words carefully. "Forgive me, Penny, but I'm guessing you already know the next bit?"

Clancy simply nodded, not wishing to interrupt her, and certainly not knowing whatever it was she was supposed to know, as she sensed something important was about to come forth.

"You belong with each other."

Clancy managed to suppress what would have been a nod just as Margaret's attention was diverted. She'd seen Arthur appearing from the kitchen with the new tray of drinks. She looked over at him and quickly said. "*No*, Arthur my love, we need clean cups too."

"What!" came the incredulous reply.

"*Yes*, be a love and get them please and then come and join us?"

Sensing that he still wasn't wanted, a man intruding on a conversation between two females with much of importance to discuss, he turned back, complete with tray, good naturedly and took his time. He re-entered the kitchen while Mariah looked on with mounting puzzlement. She could have sorted all this within seconds and she was not at all sure why her employer had been pressed into service in this way.

Margaret's speech now sped up, sensing that she had not got long to finish what bubbled within. "*So*, are you going to stay and fight for someone whom, forgive me, I *believe* you love too, or are you just going to walk away? Someone who can share that normal loving relationship." There it was, the stark and brave truth, declared and able to bear the closest of scrutiny that either woman one-to-one might care to expose it to. Furthermore, this is why Clancy had come. Sadly, it was to crystallise her thoughts irrevocably, but in the wrong direction. Even worse, without knowing it, the older woman had mentioned one little word that at a stroke swept any vestiges of hope from the younger.

"Margaret, thank you, thank you *so much* for all that, but I think this is one fight that has already been lost." For the moment she stared past the older woman as if the mist of uncertainty had finally cleared. "And, in truth, I think I'm finished fighting. It's time for me to move on."

Margaret paused again, her mouth moved but no words came, she struggled with, and almost succeeded in, hiding her disappointment and it's unhappy travelling companion – regret. She almost thought twice about saying the words that she decided to proceed with anyway, "Moving on, or running away?"

Clancy wasn't an easy woman to offend as Margaret had concluded before she spoke.

"A bit of both, I suppose, Margaret."

It was then that the older woman realised that the moment was lost to her. She conceded defeat with a slight nod accompanied only by unabridged silence and an acknowledgement that she could do no more. She needed a second or two to compose herself and looked away as she did so.

Arthur approached once again and Clancy saw Margaret shake her head ever so slightly, trying to reset her own thoughts. The older woman accepted that she had said enough and more words would either offend or damage their guest; she quickly dropped into a completely new line of conversation as if all that had gone before was spoken in a waking dream. Despite her intention to conceal it, Arthur did not miss her attempt, just as she looked away, to defeat the moisture that had precipitated in the corner of his wife's eyes.

"I've just been hearing about Penny's travel plans, Arthur." She poured Clancy a fresh cup of tea.

"Oh, my! I suspect Horizon will not be the same without you, Penny. So, have you a new job or will you just be travelling?"

"No, just travelling, Arthur. Although, of course, missions with Horizon have allowed me to see much of the world, it has always been a bit of a narrow snapshot and I always planned to do more travelling when I could just kick back and take my time. Now seems to be a good opportunity to do that."

Arthur nodded as she sipped her tea. The former agent listened while he recounted tales of the travels of his youth. His left hand was now being employed to add further emphasis to his account. Although she was polite and widened her eyes with excitement and laughed in all the right places, Margaret could tell that she was already thinking of other things. Moreover, the perceptive mother sensed there was something else; something critical had happened that had precipitated Clancy's actions now. She had no clue as to what this might be, but she did know that this had little if anything to do with her son and had much more to do with the attractive young woman whose recent decision to leave had been influenced by it – whatever it was.

A short time later their guest stood to take her leave. The sleeveless sundress with a gathered waist and flared skirt immediately fell into place around the shapely knees as she did so. For the second time that afternoon Arthur remained focussed on her and not on her legs. Sadness seemed to descend among the three of them.

"Penny, I am so sorry, *we* are so sorry to see you go. I do hope you will keep in touch?" Margaret had failed just as her words had failed; there was no more she could either say or do. She did her best to blink back a forming tear as she was reminded of their daughter who was absent from their lives through factors beyond their comprehension or control. She'd been hoping to at least save this one. Although she made a valiant attempt to do so the sadness that ran within was too great for her to contain.

Clancy hugged first Arthur then Margaret. They walked out to her car with her. It remained gleaming in the afternoon sunshine hurting their eyes as it did so. Just before she opened the car door she withdrew a small mobile device from her handbag.

"This will contact me if you need me. Just press here and I will do my best to get in touch with you. I'll always try to help you both."

One final kiss for Margaret whose eyes seemed even more moist than they had a few moments ago; another hug for Arthur and she entered the car without further delay. The restrained but throaty growl came from the engine venting through the four exhaust pipes while she traversed their drive. Finally, the speed picked up, some loose gravel crunched under the substantial tyres, as the engine was unleashed and, suddenly, she was gone. The closing gates clanged together like a subdued peal from a funeral bell signifying the end of a battle that had been lost, exacting many casualties, with only one or two remaining to bear witness to such a thing.

Margaret showed Arthur the small device, by way of the smallest of consolations to the gap that had opened within their lives. The special App glowed on screen and Margaret bit her tongue as she attempted, but failed, to limit her tears although she did manage to stifle the urge to press it at once.

Chapter IV

Loss of All Hands

Some weeks went by. News of the departure of their best and most popular colleague made it a difficult time for many of the agents and in particular Toby. He walked along lonely corridors in Horizon HQ rather like the ghost of a captain whose ship had sunk some years before, together with the entire crew, with him still at his post. He recognised that he could not have come through this time of trial without the unstinting efforts of Alexis who'd almost deserted her business in order to spend more time with him. Eventually, he made yet another attempt to try to contact Clancy, calling round to her apartment. He saw her F-Type parked in its usual spot but the dust on the windscreen indicated that it had not moved for some time. She was nowhere to be seen.

Throughout this time many changes had taken place within the Horizon organisation. All of these had been initiated by Clancy, who had conducted a thorough review before she departed. A new underground operations room had been created which ran continuously day and night. A mobile force was available for each and every mission. This meant that even assignments that were carried out in foreign lands had a backup force to call upon at a moment's notice. If the organisation were so stretched as to be unable to provide this, then new engagements were declined. Agents were encouraged to wear at all times, when on duty, a discrete communications link that allowed an agent to monitor any mission but also to contact other agents. In addition it would give off the location of any of the agents who'd activated it.

Some of the agents kept the link open continuously, even when not on active operations.

During these weeks, as winter became a distant memory and spring gave way to summer, Janet completed her training in record time. Indeed, it was widely held, but never confirmed, that she'd passed each milestone much faster than Clancy had. Not only this, but each assessment was passed with flying colours. Moreover, a fully-recovered Tim had long since re-joined and completed his training. The two agents, now very much an 'item' were invariably placed together and a string of missions were completed on time, below budget and, above all, successfully.

Rather like a mourner visiting a grave, Toby had got into the habit of monitoring each agent's location from the operations room. Although not required, the practice of leaving their comms link open had spread to those not on duty. This meant that a tiny graphic of the agent and their position could be displayed on the large screen in the 'bunker', buried below ground, that was the control room. More often than not Tim's icon and Janet's were to be found together not only on missions that had been assigned jointly to them but for most of their leisure time too.

There was another, more important, reason why Toby had descended underground in this way night after night like a concerned father waiting for his daughter to come in from a date and return the family car as she did so. This, as many of the surveillance staff quickly realised, was the fact that occasionally, just occasionally, the graphic of "MC1" would appear on screen and this would mean that Clancy had logged on to and was monitoring the agents' communications and also the mission. Such an act would give away her position and Toby would often sit at the console staring at the screen desperate to click on her icon and so activate a line of communication with her. Like a man dying of thirst espying an oasis that he knew he could not reach, he somehow managed to resist such an urge, reasoning that she had chosen to be left alone and ultimately, regardless of the limitless craving within, he had to respect her wishes. Furthermore, at first her location was within the UK but as the days passed he saw that she was now located in North America and was heading further north and west with each update.

Tim and Janet soon became the two most successful agents. They were on a mission to monitor a client's son who'd been thought to have been radicalised by a militant and extremist cleric at a mosque.   Tim and Janet were established on rooftops over the road from the mosque. A late night class was in session. It was believed that during or soon after the class the latest convert, their client's son, would be given the instruction and the means to commit an atrocity. Horizon believed that this would mean a suicide bombing.

Janet had set up her Barrett M82 sniper rifle on the flat roof facing. She'd extended the bipod, which supported the weighty front end and was checking the target with a paraphernalia of gadgets in order to secure greater accuracy for her shots. She had rejected the Accuracy International rifle as chosen by Toby and Clancy as being not powerful enough. The M82 rifle favoured by American forces took an enormous .50-calibre cartridge, which was capable, if fired repeatedly, of breaching concrete emplacements and was often used in machine guns. The energy released by the projectile and its weight of over twice that of a British AI rifle gave rise to a violent recoil that had been known to dislocate shoulders and even detach retinas in sharp-shooters. Janet was unconcerned and had slammed the 'pop guns' of Clancy and Toby as being outmoded and lacking the power needed by the serious and committed professional sniper. She always used a suppressor, which would not only give the advantage of reducing some of the force of the recoil, but also would obscure the flash and the report from the rifle as it went off. Toby, in the control room was monitoring the mission. He saw that Clancy's link was activated and it appeared that she too was eavesdropping on the conversation.

Tim was talking to Janet as she prepared her rifle. "So, I see you've set up your M82?"

"Yes, and I am also using the low light vision sight."

"So, you don't use the Schmidt and Bender sight, like Miss Clancy?" Janet bit her lower lip as if making a half-hearted attempt to restrain the words that then flowed.

"No, that's all out of date now. Nobody uses that stuff anymore. Old Pen," as she liked to refer to Clancy, "was a bit of a dinosaur. Her sight won't work in the dark, while with this one I can see what the old sod has eaten for dinner."

"And I can see you use a laser sight too, as well as a laser range finder, wind direction calculator for the windage as well as one to adjust for the fall of the shot."

"Yes, Tim we need these things to get *reliable* results. All that mumbo jumbo guff that Pen used to peddle about feeling the wind on your cheek crap, it just won't fly in today's world when we are up against professionals. This is the modern way. Old Pen's methods were at best questionable and at worse *dangerous*. Could get you killed. In fact, from what I hear, did get a few killed. How many agents did you lose; four or was it five?"

Tim remained quiet as he thought about his partner's answers.

She continued, "If she met *me*, came up against me one-to-one, I mean, then I'd show her, for the brief time that she'd remain alive, how much better a shooter I am now than she ever was. That stupid fuck would learn what it is to be a shooter not some file-your-nails-and-see-where-this-goes lightweight. Talking of old fucks, did you ever bang her?"

"*What*, me and Miss Clancy! No, we weren't like that!"

She glared at him clearly resenting the pedestal on which he'd placed the former agent. "Reckon she'd be a sad old fuck, bet good money you ain't missin' much anyways. Bet she fucked worse than her shooting."

Tim swallowed hard not having experiencing such vitriol from Janet previously and picked out from their conversation the thing that had upset him the most. "But, I've seen Miss Clancy hit some amazing targets, often at long range in severe conditions."

She moved her gaze away from the instruments, she wanted to look at him directly as she had an important point to make. "So, she had a bit of luck. That's all it was *nothing* more. Sooner or later luck runs out, that's why she's gone - realises next shoot out she won't come through. She'll be in the middle of a shit storm with nowhere to hide and that's when agents will die; sorry, that should be *more* agents will die saving her sorry ass!" She now pulled back further from her rifle so that her focus held him fully within its tawny grasp. "Look, Tim you are with *me* now, period! I am the one who saved you when she left you there bleeding to death on the sidewalk while she stripped off, flashing all her assets, such as they are," she chimed with distaste, "to go and interdict the Russian guy. It's a good job I came along or you'd have died while she went off playing at being the hero," she continued with mounting scorn, "and that took her long enough. No doubt she was too busy showing her skimpy underwear while you lay dying." She continued to glare at Tim with passion. "You guys need to wake up and smell the coffee."

Meanwhile, in the control room Toby saw Clancy's icon blink a couple of times and then it was extinguished. No doubt one or two pixels still glowed, marking her position but within a few seconds even these went dark. It was over; Clancy had gone just like her now absent icon. He touched the screen where her icon had been, a ghosting and fading image. How he wished he'd clicked on the communications link to speak with her while he could. Sadly, it was too late.

Janet had more to tell. "Remember, it was me, and only me, who saved you. That surgeon guy had thrown in the towel like the rest of them. He told me that you'd passed; it was hopeless. I told him he was to step the fuck up and be the man, not throw you under the bus. Boy, did I give him both barrels. Only then did he shape up." Hazel eyes narrowed as they continued to stare at him, until he nodded, seeking some relief from their constant gaze.

Toby couldn't help but wonder what Miss Clancy would have thought of Janet's exposition. In his opinion she'd done the only thing possible in neutralising the Russian assassin otherwise none of them nor any of the medical crew would have been able to approach. If Clancy had not intervened he'd have been able to bring fire on all of them and Toby doubted whether any of them would have been spared from the shots of such an indiscriminate killer. Now more than ever he wanted to click her communication link but it had long since faded into the ether and was no longer available to him. This vignette illustrated his dilemma; things had happened so fast with Clancy. It was all he could do to ensure the prosecution of her ex-foster parents and next to no discussion had taken place with her as regards her future or her plans. Indeed, there were so many things to tell her, so many important things to voice, to ask and to offer. As he stared at the place where her icon had stopped glowing, he realised that he may never have a chance even to use a disparate electronic link, let alone his favoured option of seeing her face-to-face. His thoughts, once again, were broken by Janet's voice.

"Look, there's the car! And look through the upstairs window; that's the preacher-of-hate, Imam guy. I'm gonna take him out. So long bad ass!"

"Are you sure Janet, what if you have the wrong one and you kill an innocent chap – inside a mosque? The riots would run for days."

"Look, Tim, shooting this fucker would be a kindness to our fellow men."

Mercifully, the team would never know what the consequences would be for in that moment, as her finger itched against the trigger, the front door opened. The young man in flowing robes appeared and walked hesitantly as if carrying unaccustomed weight and apparatus to the recently arrived car.

"Look that's him!" called Tim. "His robes are bulging and that's a trigger in his hand." He spoke into his microphone just after pressing the button on the radio that allowed him to communicate with anti-terrorist forces. "All units respond, target is on the move. Close in now. Approach with caution and assume subject is wired for explosives."

Tim fired immediately into the wooden door, causing it to be slammed shut. Meanwhile Janet began firing at the waiting car. The first massive shell destroyed the engine as it gave up immense kinetic energy as the projectile was arrested. The Barrett went off causing a brutal kick that caused the bipod gun mounting to rise up violently despite the suppressor and Janet's muscular right shoulder making an attempt to restrain it. Her second destroyed the front tyre, which caused the whole wheel to lurch at an odd angle. The third shot, reserved similar treatment for the rear wheel. A terrified driver attempted to get out of the car, holding his arms up as he did so. Janet fired again, the shell destroying his right shoulder and caused his arm to now flap oddly at his side. Surgeons would struggle for months to save his right arm let alone his right shoulder. His dominant arm would be forever weakened.

Toby heard her say, "Take that sucker!" just before the shot was despatched.

Security forces now massed and had blocked the road and sealed off all the streets around the mosque. All of them had combat gear on and two had bomb-proof tunics. A loud megaphone called to the young man.

"One more step and we'll shoot you. Do not attempt to come forwards; this is your only warning. Take your robes off now, do it, do it now and then kneel on the floor. Do it and do it now."

The young man looked dazed but did as he was told in a frenzy of activity. The suicide vest was revealed to all present. The wired trigger now dangled from his right wrist.

"Take the vest off, and place it beside you on the pavement. Do it and do it now!"

Once again he complied.

As the vest was laid on the ground a tracked robot was activated and whirred insistently as it came towards him. The vest had numerous pockets all stuffed with ball-bearings and coils of explosives laced with nails.

"Get up and take your shirt off and raise your arms. Do it or we *will* shoot you."

As soon as this was done and the anti-terrorist squad could see that he was hiding nothing further, more words came forth.

"Walk forwards slowly, keep your arms above your head. Do it now! Do not attempt to touch the vest or we will fire without further warning."

Once again he complied, Tim could see through his Schmidt and Bender optical sight the tears streaming down his face.

The robot continued onwards, its lights, cameras and long arm extending in front of it as it did so. The young man and the robot passed each other as both went in opposite directions. Men came forward pointing Sig Sauer assault rifles at him as walked unhappily towards the anti-terrorist forces.

"Stop, kneel," one shouted.

As soon as he'd carried out this instruction men came forwards to apprehend him.

They then called to the driver; his arm and much of the floor was covered in blood. He came forwards to vacate the danger zone. The wail of an approaching ambulance could be heard as he did so. Meanwhile the robot continued forwards and as the men withdrew to a safe distance taking their prisoner with them, a controlled charge was set off to destroy the vest.

Tim looked over at Janet and nodded towards the driver who was still nursing his shattered arm, "Why did you shoot him, he was surrendering?"

"Look, Tim, I believe you lost five agents to those two Russian bastards, all in surrender situations. How many agents do you want to lose? The last mother fucker nearly killed you. 'Shoot first, then ask questions later' will keep you and me alive. If you'd followed my strategy then you would'na been in that Goddamned mess. The men you left behind in the groundnut warehouse in Niger were the ones who identified you all."

"No, Janet it was the CCTV footage and our South Africa trip."

"Really! Seriously! Need I say more?" She glared at him now and then began nodding her head as if making him a future promise. "When *I'm* in charge we'll do things very differently."

Tim swallowed so hard that she was able to detect the nervousness on his face.

"Only joking, Tim," she offered, but Tim wondered if she was.

"Come on let's go. I need my post mission drink and fuck."

She picked up the M82 and held an arm out towards him as he was replacing his AI rifle in its transport case, as Clancy had taught him.

"Look, stow that piece of shit and let's go. I'm feeling thirsty and horny and not necessarily in that order."

Tim clicked the locks on the oblong case retaining his specially modified AI rifle and as soon as he'd done so he ran to catch up with her as they vacated the roof.

Toby remained in the operations room. This wasn't the way Clancy would have run things. He vainly tried to identify the now dark pixels that had previously glowed with her presence. Their dark reply only served to clarify his sense of loss even more. How he missed her. He wondered what she thought of Janet's tirade against her and her methods. Maybe now he would never know.

Later that night Toby was in communication via a secure link with Dame Helen.

"Another wonderful operation successfully concluded, Mr Richmond. Once again Her Majesty's Government is indebted to you and your organisation. It seems we have come to rely on your discreet, precise and careful intervention more and more. I see that we are calling you now on a regular basis."

"Indeed, Dame Helen."

"I am so pleased that we were able to assist you with Mr Mdombku. I am told the very same day his sponsor Mr Romanonov suffered a fatal heart attack."

"Yes, Ma'am, I am told it was a particularly nasty one."

"Yes, I believe so, Mr Richmond. How fortuitous for your organisation. It seems, too, that since that time you have gone from strength to strength and no doubt we shall continue to rely on you and your services. Just one tiny criticism if I may?" Her voice was charged, he recognised that all that had come before was preamble.

"Ma'am?"

"Many of your current operations, whilst concluded satisfactorily, seem to lack the finesse that we'd come to expect from you and your colleague, Miss Clancy. The driver shot tonight was just that; a simple driver in the wrong place. His arm is so badly damaged that it will require months of restorative surgery and will attract significant payment also exposure to HM Government that we are trying to limit. This is *why* we are calling upon Horizon."

"Yes, I understand Dame Helen."

"Where is Miss Clancy, I am told she is no longer with you?"

"That is correct Ma'am."

"Well, Mr Richmond if I might be permitted to say, her absence has been noted and this is a great shame. My department, as you know, is charged with overseeing delicate and subtle operations that we seem to have a regular need of and yet one of your best agents is no longer with you."

"She is sorely missed by us all Ma'am."

"Good heavens *man*, can you not simply go and get her, wherever she is?"

It was unusual for their sponsor to comment in this way. In the previous two years of regular contact she had not voiced similar concerns.

"It isn't for want of trying, Dame Helen. It seems that she no longer wishes to be found."

"I very much doubt that, Mr Richmond. Our advice, if you'd permit me, is for you to do whatever is required in order to secure her return."

Toby thought that it was typical of the Minister to make advice sound more like a directive. "I shall do my best with that, ma'am."

"Very good. I will settle your invoice in full and the Treasury will be instructed to effect the transfer first thing in the morning. If I may, I will withhold your usual bonus on this occasion. The wounded driver will need months of reconstructive surgery on his shoulder and it will be both expensive and will need further measures to keep it out of the public eye. We have had to admit him to the specialist unit at the Queen Elizabeth Hospital in Birmingham where we have our secure unit, but such things are not ideal; placing him next to injured troops."

"Of course, Dame Helen, I understand."

"Goodnight then, Mr Richmond. Get Miss Clancy back with all speed."

"Dame Helen."

He closed the link a little deflatedly. Although Horizon was evidently still on the preferred list, she was giving him fair warning. Indeed, this was the closest she'd come to an admonishment. She rarely commented at all about their methods as long as the outcome was a favourable one. Moreover, the Minister had previously and habitually been happy to include huge bonuses as their invoice was settled. Even worse than all of those things was that Toby couldn't help but agree with her. Janet, at the outset, was a quiet and respectful woman who seemed to be a perfect fit with Tim's quiet nature. Sadly, as time had passed and her confidence had grown it had brought out many more distasteful attributes.

It was to be just after midnight, a couple of nights later as Toby had lingered in the bunker. Clancy's icon appeared on the almost deserted screen as many operations had concluded and most agents had turned in for the night. As it glowed at him, like an old friend, it gave off her position as she journeyed north, to Chicago and then west towards either Seattle or Canada and Vancouver. Then the link suddenly went dark and somehow, deep inside, he knew that it henceforth would remain so.

CHAPTER V

Failed Recovery

A few days later Toby left Horizon HQ for a week's holiday. All in the organisation were surprised by this news because he'd left Alexis behind and as the two had long become inseparable, this only served to raise people's curiosity still further. He boarded a direct flight from Manchester to Chicago and, after making enquiries there, boarded another direct flight to Vancouver. He hired a car in Vancouver and the following day drove north to Horseshoe Bay and on to the ferry bound for Nanaimo on Vancouver Island. He stayed overnight in Nanaimo and then drove west early the following morning. Late morning he parked just in front of a log cabin on the edge of the Pacific Rim National Park and, after double-checking the information he'd uncovered, he walked up the short track to the front door. He couldn't help but notice the wonderful views over the Pacific Ocean and north to Tofino. The warm westerly tousled his hair comprehensively as he waited.

She came to the door after an unusually long delay. Prior to this he could have sworn that he heard a heavy glass object, which he recognised as being a spirit bottle, hit the wooden floor. He did his best to hide the shock he felt at the change in her appearance.

"You could get eaten by bears out here, Clancy, and nobody would ever know."

"Yes, not only have they worked out how to get into the bear-proof bins but they have even worked out which day they are collected. Still, they make for good target practice!"

He looked horrified.

"Only joking, Toby. So, how did you find me?"

"I started in Chicago, which was the last place I had a definite signal from your communicator." Clancy nodded as he spoke, but there was an unusual detached look in her eyes that he'd never noticed before, throughout the time that he'd known her. "I had noticed on one or two nights when I was in the operations room that your communications link had been activated. I just happened to be in there," he lied, choosing not to tell her that he'd been focussed on such events for weeks. "From Chicago I looked at the flight manifests and saw your name appearing, bound for Vancouver. Then, it was a matter in Vancouver of checking with the car hire services. I had a chat with the chap who hired you the blue compact you have out there. That's the thing about being such an attractive person Clancy, people remember you. He remembered that you'd asked about the ferry to Vancouver Island. From there it was simply a matter of checking with the realtors in Nanaimo and here we are." A long pause opened and he knew that his feelings of concern for her would appear on his expression any moment. Mercifully he looked down at his left hand, thereby distracting her and mainly himself.

"Happy birthday, Clancy!"

He kissed her and handed over the carefully wrapped present he carried, with a silver bow that had become a little crumpled with the journey. "Alexis chose it and as you'll be able to tell, she wrapped it too."

Clancy set the present down to open later.

"Thank you and please thank her? Can I get you a drink, Toby?"

At this point Toby couldn't help but notice the empty bottles of gin that were piling up in the recycling bin. What was more, he had smelt the tell-tale odour of the stale spirit on her breath and also on her as he'd come close to her.

"No, I'm fine thanks, Clancy. I just wanted to see how you were and also to invite you to our wedding early next year. I have reserved a place for you." He saw the likely refusal forming on her expression and decided to try to pre-empt it. "Perhaps don't give me a definite answer now but maybe think about it? You know we'll keep your invite open and if you turn up, that will be an extra special bonus." Once again the most awkward of pauses opened.

"You couldn't have chosen somewhere a bit nearer, Penny?"

"I just fancied a complete break."

"Well you have certainly got that; I think only New Zealand or Easter Island, perhaps, would have been further."

"I tried those places but there were no bears."

"Mm well, you have clearly made a big impression on them, judging by those bins out there.

I also wanted to tell you that your ex foster parent has been sent away for twenty years. He was found to be a serious threat to women and the judge has insisted that he serve his term out. We wanted even longer and pushed for this but apparently this was the longest term the judge could give. I'm told a warm reception awaits him in prison. I suspect it should keep him awake most nights if the guilt does not! I hope you got my email about him?"

She nodded. "Thank you, Toby, I am so pleased that he has his just desserts after all this time. I am sorry I could not have acted sooner."

"Don't give that a second thought Penny, we are through this now and it's his turn to reflect on things. His wife has stuck by him so it looks as though she may have known all along what he was up to."

"Yes, it doesn't surprise me. So much went on in that house right under the noses of social services. She must have been in on it from start to finish."

"Well, it's certainly finished, social services are being investigated."

Clancy nodded as she registered his words. On a deeper and more punitive plane she recognised that she could only blame herself. Surely it was all her fault. She knew now that only another drink would make the guilt go away.

"You are looking well Toby, must be Alexis' influence."

"Thanks, Penny, and so are you," he lied. In point of fact, Clancy was looking dreadful.

She brought him a cup of tea and he couldn't help but notice the shaking hand as she set it down on the small table in front of him. Much of the tea spilt into the saucer. It was only by continuing to speak that he was able to obscure some of the concern and shock he held over her appearance.

"You left in such a hurry, there was no time to finalise anything. There were so many things I wanted to go through with you; so many things to say." A pause in his speech was about to open again; he knew only that he had to avoid this. He grasped for more words. "You'll have a generous pension in perpetuity. If you choose never to work again, then you'll still be comfortable. Although you are a lot younger than the usual Horizon retiree, the benefits will still apply to you and will continue to do so. Your flat is fully paid and your car remains yours to keep. I've asked someone to drive it for an hour a month, so as to protect the car and the engine."

She seemed totally disinterested in what happened to her car. Her former pride and joy, it had always been kept spotless, unlike the sad and dusty monument to past times she'd almost discarded in her parking spot.

While he sipped his tea, she produced a tall glass with a colourless liquid in which he assumed was a large neat gin. It was still early and the way she consumed it seemed more out of dependence than a social pleasure. His words had stopped as he stared just for a moment. Unhappy thoughts rushed within and he could only hope that such would not appear on his expression; how much the young woman, his friend, had deteriorated and how quickly.

He asked a question to which he already knew the answer. "If you'd like to return as a non-field agent, then we can make you that offer too?"

"I can't go back, Toby. Did you come here to get me to return with you?"

He paused before forming a reply. His instinctive response was not based on any form of words at all and he nearly gave vent to it by scooping her up in his arms and carrying her from the purgatory in which, somehow, she'd placed herself. Having done that, he'd not let go of her until she was safe among those who simply thought the world of her – those who would have been greatly distressed, as he was, to see her in this place in this condition.

Ultimately, it was the recollection of the look upon her face that day that they'd had that terrible row, where she'd with one almighty sweep from her arms overturned a large glazed cabinet. Remembering that look now, where she'd unequivocally sent signals that she hated him, his life and everything he'd done for her, threw him off centre before he could even move, and disastrously so. For he'd learned after that time that such a reaction was really a reflection of hatred for herself and not for him. Something of her look now, as she posed her question, had reminded him of this and he knew that his only recourse was to pull back until such time as she was ready to confront those issues – or, more likely, he could do the same.

"No, not really, Penny. I just wanted to see you to pass you some forms and to make sure you had everything you need and, of course, to wish you a happy birthday." His words hung in the air and each of them knew there were more that must follow. It was time for him to acknowledge the truth rather than hope for a different outcome. "Penny, I can see that you are not well enough to return. I can see that your Horizon days are over. You will always be the best agent I've ever seen, although I can now accept that events have moved on. I accept what you say."

"And Janet?" She bit her lip as she said the name.

"Oh, she is a very different proposition and though she gets the job done it's at a very high price. She tends to lack the finesse, shall I say, and tends to be a bit trigger-happy. She certainly takes no prisoners in the full sense of that word."

Clancy's expression became glazed; surely such considerations were to do with another person in a former life. One final thought crystallised in his brain and having done so he knew that he just had to voice it. She deserved no less.

"I promise I can see there is no point in trying to get you to return, if you have moved on. I just didn't want you to disappear and never be seen again. Not after everything we've been through quite apart from Horizon and I never thought you'd end up so far away from me."

She nodded, initially she seemed a little surprised, but then her attention was subsumed by the drink in her hand, which she greedily consumed as if her life depended upon it. Of all the words and actions that day this one vignette served to confirm the belief that she was not fit and was far from being so. Most likely, she would never be fit. He rose to go.

"Are you going to stay over, I can make a bed up for you?"

He wondered judging by the state of the place if this were true.

"No thanks, Penny, I'm booked in at the Grand Pacific in Victoria and it's a long drive south. I am flying straight back from Vancouver in the morning." At this point he could no longer maintain eye-contact; her present state distressed him too much for him to do so. He certainly could not divulge that he'd booked two rooms in Victoria as well as two flight tickets. The shock was overtaking him again and in so doing it disabled his decision making process. He knew he had to have time to think, to re-plot it. In addition, such was the distress now mounting within that he knew he had to get away, at least for now. He kissed her; once again, he noted the unmistakeable smell of gin. All he could do, as always, was to seek refuge in repetition and small talk. He set the forms he'd brought with him down on the little table. He wondered if she would ever look at them, let alone post them. How things had changed, how she'd changed.

"Clancy, you will always have a friend in me and you will always have a home in Manchester, quite apart from Horizon.

Will you think about the wedding, as we'd both love to see you there?"

She kissed him and as he turned to leave she once again looked at her empty glass and wondered if it was time to refill it. Toby walked down the short trail and found his parked car. As he drove south he phoned Alexis. He could defeat neither the concern nor sorrow in his voice. He was shaking and was grateful that Alexis could not see him, although she'd detected the trembling in his voice.

"Poor Clancy is finished. Sad to say, she's switched from counting successful missions to counting gin bottles – empty gin bottles. She's not fit for a haircut let alone an active agent's role."

"Oh *no*, and you left her there?"

"What else could I do? I couldn't *make* her come back with me."

"Is there *any way* we can help her, we can't just leave her there, Toby, on the other side of the world."

"Not unless she says she wants help."

"But we can't leave her out there all alone! I should have come with you."

"Oh no, we won't do that but, for now, unless and until she wants help or she's ready to come back. I also think her agent days are over. She had trouble pouring a cup of tea; her hands were shaking so much. I am afraid the whole place was strewn with empty gin bottles. I certainly don't think she'll ever get back to handling a sniper rifle again."

"We can't leave it like that, Toby. We can't leave *her* like that."

"We won't I promise, but I'm just not sure at the moment what I can do. I need to think. I can't force her to come with me."

"Very well then, Toby, you fly back and we can have a chat about the best way of helping her. Or maybe I can fly out and meet you; we'll both go and try to persuade her and let's get her back here."

"Yes, good idea. I need to get back. I have just one mission to close and as soon as it's done then let's both fly back and see what we can do together?"

"Oh okay then, as soon as you have sorted this mission, suppose we both fly back to Vancouver Island and I vote we don't leave without her, is that agreed?"

"That's wonderful Alexis, thank you. I do love you."

"I suspect recovering Penny will be your hardest mission but I promise you won't be doing it alone. I'll clear some space in my diary and, as soon as we can, we travel back to Canada and begin our save Clancy mission."

"Goodnight my love."

"I'll see you as soon as you fly in to Manchester."

"Yes I'm on the next flight."

He silenced the call with a quick prod of his phone. Once again he was reminded, not that such a thing was needed, of all the reasons why he loved Alexis so much.

CHAPTER VI

Constant Surveillance

No sooner had Toby reached his hotel room on the waterfront at Victoria than he noticed that his laptop was beeping with an incoming Skype call. As usual, the transmission was scrambled with a 24 bit digital overlay, which prevented eavesdropping. He knew, however, who was making such a call before he pressed the respond button.

"Dame Helen, good evening."

"Oh yes, Mr Richmond, your office said you were away. It's a bright sunny morning here in London." Her perfunctory attempt at affability dispensed with, she continued, "Look, we have a tricky situation that has come to my attention and I have put Horizon forward as being the best of our covert operatives to handle it. I must confess that there are some in my department who are very unhappy over recent events. I am afraid it looks like the driver may lose his arm after all, Mr Richmond, and I am under pressure to cancel further operations and choose more in-house solutions. It could be a terrible embarrassment for the Government."

It didn't take too long for Toby to work out whose embarrassment was most likely in the offing. He kept his responses to the minimum, which was always a good idea when talking with the Minister. "I see, Dame Helen."

"Well, for now I have managed to get my superiors to agree to what we hope is a limited surveillance mission. It came to our attention within the last twenty-four hours that several persons on our watched list coming from North Korea had flown in to London. This was under the auspices of a trade delegation but as you know our trade with North Korea is virtually non-existent. We can't understand why all of a sudden the North Koreans have sent one such now. Again, as I am sure you know, they are tricky customers and quite unpredictable. Our feeling is that they could, well, do just about anything. The whole country is unstable. The Americans tried to bribe them with food and resources but they flatly refused to give up their nuclear programme; then they tried to blackmail Uncle Sam, which is never a clever thing to do. They've been letting off missiles like it's Guy Fawkes day." Toby did his best to keep a straight face as she struggled to get her plummy accent round such words.

She went on, not having noticed his attempts to do so. "We believe the trade delegation is a *ruse* to get up to a dozen of their agents into the UK for purposes of which, frankly, we are not too sure. We want each and every one of these people to be followed discreetly and then we'd like a report as to *why* they are here. Or, at the very least, we'd like to know *where* they go. It must be something quite important for the North Koreans to go to all this trouble – we haven't heard a peep out of them for over a decade, so *something* must be in the offing. The other interesting thing is that we would not have spotted them at all going through immigration control if it were not for the fact that they have all had work done."

"Work, Dame Helen?"

"Yes, the shape of their eyes has been surgically altered. We believe this is solely for the purpose of their blending in. We are not quite sure why this should be so or what importance, if any, we should attach to this, *but* we need to find out; or rather, we need *you* to find out. One of our eagle eyed immigration officers, and thank heavens we still have one or two of those, noted that there was a disparity between our pictures on file, the images in their passports and their new physical appearance. Certainly, no trade delegation would go to such trouble to make their members' features fit in with a typical British Caucasian appearance. We believe that they are planning something big. Their numbers, the recent appearance when things have been quiet for so long and their oculoplastic surgery mean they want to be *unobtrusive*. This can *only* mean some important covert operation.

So, Mr Richmond, what we are asking Horizon to do is to follow them discreetly. I am afraid it will mean that you must be at your most careful as we do not want them to know they are under observation, as it may then spoil our chances of discovering *why* they are here. We need to know this with some urgency. Two further things apply. I am afraid unless you can come through with your former minimal casualty rates and provide us with discreet, but all-encompassing, surveillance then we will not be partaking of Horizon's services again. By all means report directly to me if you wish or you can always contact Melissa, my PA. Finally, I must ask that you begin immediately or at least as soon as you are back in the UK."

"I understand Dame Helen. We will do our best not to let you down. Thank you for giving us this opportunity to redeem ourselves." Toby's expression turned grave as he blinked back in the web cam.

"Good luck, Mr Richmond. Lastly, is there any news of Miss Clancy?"

"Only that, regrettably Ma'am, she isn't fit enough to return."

"I am sorry to hear that. I am of the view that things have slipped, shall I say, in your organisation since she departed. I'd better let you get some sleep I think you'll be in the thick of things as soon as you get back. It's a shame Miss Clancy is not available as I suspect she would have been ideally suited to a mission of this type."

"Indeed, Ma'am."

"I've prepared a file with more information. Would you be so kind as to collect it from my office the day after tomorrow? Shall we say ten, UK time? Good day, Mr Richmond."

"Very well, Ma'am."

She terminated the link with no further pleasantries. Indeed, as was her wont, there may have been a polite veneer to some of her requests but Toby considered that such requests amounted to more a list of orders, that he would be wise to execute both without question and as soon as possible or as requested. Toby immediately went online to see if he could switch his flight from one that came in via Manchester to one that flew in to Heathrow. He also phoned Brady to see if he could assemble a team that would be ready to make a start as soon as he was in receipt of some more details.

It was perhaps unsurprising that Toby caught very little sleep that night. Dame Helen's sponsorship had brought a raft of missions that were lucrative and had nearly always attracted significant bonuses – until now. Moreover, the cases were generally easy to accomplish and could often be finalised quickly. The things that HM Government were looking for had, hitherto, been easy to deliver – discretion and subtlety. By such means Toby had been able to rebuild Horizon, attract new recruits and put something of their recent setbacks behind them. Inevitably, this triggered more thoughts about Clancy and the dragging miserable feeling he felt inside that he knew would persist until he managed to resolve her predicament, which was made so much worse by his visiting her. This in turn triggered doubts about the performance of their ex-barista who, as her confidence had grown, displayed a steady diminution of things such as discretion and subtlety. In fact 'bull in a china shop' seemed to describe her methods quite nicely and a wry smile came to him as he corrected his own thoughts to '*armed* bull in a china shop'.

He boarded the next flight back to the UK and, after diverting via London to pick up the confidential files Dame Helen had prepared for him, he returned to Manchester. Later the same day he held a meeting with Brady who had taken over some of the mission planning following Clancy's departure. Tim and Janet were also present.

"Okay team, we have a couple of really crucial missions."

He began by turning to their latest recruit.

"Janet, we have a money laundering operation going on in London and Monty and Miss McCready could do with another operative. Could I impose on you to get down there and help them? Here is a dossier of information. If you take the train you can read it as you travel.

I'll provide you with some outline details and then perhaps get going?"

Toby went through the case details carefully with her. As soon as Janet had been provided with enough information, she rose and vacated the meetings room. She seemed bitterly disappointed when Toby informed her that she wouldn't need her firearm. At no time did she guess that he was deliberately moving her out of the picture, at least for the time being.

The surveillance mission, passed to them via Dame Helen, called for a delicate touch. She'd made no bones about the fact that the whole organisation and their likelihood of further favour was on trial. He couldn't risk Janet intervening with guns blazing and blowing the whole operation and thereby alerting the Koreans or, even worse, gunning them down. Toby knew that Brady and Tim were more suited to lead a careful and covert surveillance mission. Tim looked carefully at Toby as he spoke with the female agent. He knew that if he had concerns about her, then he would discuss these in private with her. Both male agents sensed the deliberate ploy that Toby had put in place, but his carefully pitched expression gave no more evidence as to such a thing.

Toby then provided further details regarding their latest mission and also underlined its importance to future work of the Horizon team. Both nodded as he clarified the delicate and restrained touch that would be needed to ensure success.

"In truth, it should be a simple surveillance; the only trouble is that we are under pressure. Dame Helen basically tells me that we are drinking in the last chance saloon and if we mess this up then we won't be given any more drinks in any saloon; at least a Government-sponsored one. Given that we have predicated our expansion on a steady stream of covert operations coming from them, means we are a little exposed if suddenly it is taken away from us. I am hoping, therefore, that the two of you are the ones to lead this operation. You will need many of our agents to provide sufficient cover and rotations around the clock. It is vital that we are not exposed by the North Koreans as this will be a catastrophe for the mission and of course all at Horizon. Janet will join Monty and Karen in London but I am going to suggest we throw everything at this in order that we come through without incident. Our aim, as you realise, is to monitor very closely a dozen people who are in the UK for reasons which are uncertain. We then report back to HM Government and presumably they will deal with it from there. We are only going to be given one chance and this is it." He aimed his controller in the direction of one of the large wall-mounted screens, which flared with the first image within a few seconds.

"We believe these are our subjects." One by one he displayed the dozen photos. He made a circular motion with the laser pointer around the first subject's eyes. "You will see that all twelve, the eight men and four women have had plastic surgery, mainly around their eyes. We believe this is so that they can fit in, disappear without anyone noticing anything unusual. We are not quite sure why this is but they have gone to a lot of trouble and we need to know to what end. It's likely that they will disappear as soon as they are able. They certainly won't want to draw attention to themselves, which is why we need to move on it immediately, tonight if possible. Once they have split up, armed with new identities, then they are going to be hard to spot. For the first night they all stayed in a Travel Lodge just north of Heathrow. They then hired three cars. Surveillance provided by MI5 lost them at this point, blaming lack of manpower. This has given us an opportunity. We have their number plates being run through the ANPR computers so that we can, hopefully, find them for now but we think they will put changes in pretty quickly so time is of the essence. Their strategy will be to fade into the background over the next day or two. Jenkins has logged on to a feed from national number plate recognition systems and will alert us as soon as one of them flags up the licence plates we are looking for.

We don't know what sleeper resources they can call upon, if any, and whether they have safe houses. I suspect they will change their identities then split up and use low cost hotels in order to avoid suspicion. At all times they will strive to keep a low profile. This must be why they have had their appearances altered. A dozen North Koreans would be too memorable. They will therefore split up, blend in, then disappear only to regroup as they undertake their mission. We need to follow them. I am relying on you two to head it up. Jenkins and I will work twelve-hour shifts in the bunker if need be to ensure smooth co-ordination and free up sufficient manpower to be diverted to this mission. If you could begin at once, as soon as I have more information as regards their current whereabouts I will pass it to you."

Few questions remained and after a short interval both men nodded their heads in agreement. "We understand, Toby, we won't let you down," came from Tim.

Brady then spoke, "Tim and I will activate the team tonight and begin surveillance as soon as we can. It's only a matter of time before the cars trigger a number plate recognition device. I will inform the Police that they are not to be stopped. No effort will be spared and if they want to blend in, then that's *exactly* what we will do – while we *watch* them closely."

One of the number plate recognition computers was pinged by a car being driven by the North Koreans later that night on the M1. Brady and Tim went to work immediately.

The following two weeks saw just about every Horizon agent being pressed into service; even the mobile force had to be committed. Toby had promised when he'd set it up that it would only be called upon in the most extreme of circumstances. Without doubt, it was easy to follow someone but sooner or later the pursuer would be seen and recognised as such. For this reason the surveillance needed lots of people to pass in and out of the pursuit, which was at all times at a discreet distance, but yet never let them, any of them, out of sight. Toby realised that if they failed this assignment then there would be far fewer missions, without doubt. The dozen North Koreans soon split into six pairs. Horizon was there every step of the way as they changed their identities, means of payment and their mobile phones. A succession of rental cars and low-cost hotels were chosen and the groups split up very quickly, each of the pairs going a different direction.

Horizon were at their most resourceful throughout this period with agents taking on different roles and with rotating shifts so that round-the-clock surveillance could be put in place on all twelve of them. From the control room a variety of covers and disguises were put in place to hide at all times the true identity of the Horizon agents and, most vitally, not trigger any suspicions in the North Koreans. The fact that they'd all split up meant that Horizon needed multiple teams in order to follow them all. Mercifully the North Koreans split into six pairs rather than twelve individuals which would have necessitated even more agents working through the rotas in order to have eyes on all of them at all times. The team noted that the North Koreans all had large cameras round their necks and posed as tourists and yet never seemed to actually take any photographs.

Toby, too, applied himself with energy and enthusiasm. For a while this diverted some of his thoughts as regards Clancy and the gaping worries over her health. Purely at a subliminal level, he realised that if they could settle this mission quickly then he and Alexis could set about recovering her.

Horizon agents kept a constant log, that was updated by the personnel who were actively following their subjects, and this was available in real time to those who were about to be brought in. At no time did the foreign agents guess that they were constantly under surveillance. Regular video footage was taken covertly. A complete itinerary was sent on a constant basis, together with the video images, to Horizon's sponsors and employers so that they were fully informed of the situation. Most impressive was the planning rota that Toby sent out on a continuous basis so that each agent knew where

he or she would be required to join the pursuit and another
stood down. After an initial false start where the North Korean
agents seemed to wander in a random and haphazard pattern,
it became clear, as the days passed, that they were all
journeying both north and west, soon crossing the border into
Wales.

CHAPTER VII

Need To Know Basis

After a few days Dame Helen contacted Toby. Even more so than usual she kept any preamble and the voicing of pleasantries to a minimum and came straight to the point.

"Mr Richmond, I would like to offer my congratulations. I have seen and read the reports that have been sent into my department in a steady stream. Such detailed and varied surveillance must have weighed very heavily on your resources. The other point is that my observers are of the view that our visitors at no time were aware that they have been under constant monitoring. I can only guess at the work and diligent attention to detail that this must have entailed. I am *impressed*, well done and please accept my thanks."

"Not at all, Ma'am, it's the least we could do after our recent failings. Moreover, we were aware of the importance of the mission that you had kindly assigned to us and we were keen to give of our best. As you can see from my preliminary findings, it looks as though their trip here is a low-key, innocent one. If you would care to look at the last report we have just sent through, Ma'am it looks as though they are all headed for Anglesey!"

Dame Helen looked away from him on the secure video link. The pause that came next was of such length that Toby wondered if his laptop had frozen. Just when he was about to attempt to reboot it, she re-joined their conversation.

"Yes, Mr Richmond, I have it here. I am afraid this is very bad news."

Toby's eyes stared and his eyebrows lifted as the surprise hit him.

"Really, Ma'am, I thought much of the island was below sea level, covered in grass, full of tourists and sheep farms. I was fully expecting that you'd be asking us to stand down at this point?"

"No, Mr Richmond. How I wish that were true! I am grateful for the work you have all put in and we are all very mindful of the efforts both you and your team have brought to bear. If I may say, it has assuaged our doubts about your fitness to operate at this level and your finishing abilities, thrown into doubt since Miss Clancy departed. You have reassured us in every way."

Suddenly, her mood changed and her expression took on a grave appearance.

"Sadly, this represents our worst fears. I take it you are alone, Mr Richmond?"

"Yes indeed, Ma'am, as always when we have these conversations." Toby knew that her words were redundant, it was a condition of the secure line, and his latitude to contact her directly, that Toby was always alone when such conversations took place and also that their content was never discussed with others without prior agreement.

"I don't know if you are aware of the problems we have had since the decline of the British Advanced Gas-Cooled Reactors, which never fulfilled their potential as an alternative to the American Pressurised-Water Reactors?"

"Ma'am?"

Toby looked incredulously at the Minister. He wondered if the recent delay, while she looked down at his latest report meant that he had missed an entirely different conversation about another mission, unrelated to the one in hand. He stared, doing his best to hide the bewilderment that now started to overtake him. He failed to see what relevance there could possibly be to the current mission: one that he was fully expecting to be stood down from imminently. Furthermore, he was not aware that she had such knowledge and was so well versed in nuclear power generation. It seemed that Dame Helen revealed constant surprises whenever she had occasion to contact him. He was about to be surprised even more and he found himself nodding vigorously, his mouth having fallen open a little as more information came to light from the Minister.

"You may also know that HM Government sought to bring the French in from Électicité de France in order to construct at least two new nuclear plants. Although EDF were at first very enthusiastic, they wanted financial guarantees before they would commit to such large-scale projects. We, in turn, sought help from China who agreed, in exchange for a key role in construction and also a sharing of the expertise which the French reluctantly agreed to, to underwrite the whole project with massive funding which, frankly, would have bankrupted the entire country if we'd had to finance it without third-party assistance.

What, too, is not widely known with the failure of dash for gas and the decline of coal, mainly because of CO_2 targets, we are suffering a marked fall off in generation capacity. If the lights do not go out this coming winter then they will *surely* do so next. At this point, I am sure I do not have to remind you of your signing and adherence to the Official Secrets Act?"

"Yes Ma'am, I mean, indeed, no Ma'am."

"Domestic lights going out, let alone factories standing idle, could *topple* a government. As you might expect, this has given cause for concern in the upper echelons, should I say. The really bad news came when the French said their expected delivery schedule had slipped by some twenty years. Twenty years for God's sake! They blamed Brexit, the turmoil in French politics – everything! We are doing our best to pile into natural gas generation but our construction programme and the attempt to cap CO_2 emissions have run into failure. We tried to bring in the wind turbines but, also, what is not widely known is that these have been an expensive flop. They produce electricity only within a narrow band of conditions and much of the time it's either not windy enough or *too* windy. How can it be too windy, for God's sake? The other problem we have had is that they need expensive and round-the-clock maintenance just to keep them functioning at all. It seems the bigger they are the more problematic they become. If I hear another person tell me one of those bloody blades, that are as long as a Jumbo jet, has cracked I will scream. They may make for good photo opportunities and articles in regional newspapers, but when it comes down to actually giving off some *juice* they are a bit of a let down.

Solar showed promise especially with the fall in price of the solar panels and the Chinese were all set to dump them by the million on the west. We planned to complain at the highest level while our procurement agency quietly bought as many as we could get our hands on. We had a company lined up, Bluefield Solar, to start planting the panels by the thousand in fields. The problem is when it goes dark we need an effective means of *storing* the power. Elon Musk, the head of Tesla, has built a gigantic battery factory but we are not sure even a sizeable procurement will allow us to store enough power to get us through a bad winter, especially with other countries also beating a path to his door.

Dyson are building a research plant on an old airfield, which will research battery technology, but Sir James informs us that all of this will be applied to electric vehicles. Therein presents the next problem. With the move away from fossil fuels it seems all of a sudden everyone is producing electric cars or self-driving cars. What we then have to do is factor in the additional electricity needs this will create. The damn things may not run on petrol but they will all need to be plugged in. We simply need more power, reliable and constant power, than we have. Meanwhile, we have been shackled by our commitment to reduce CO_2 emissions. Biomass is showing some promise but we cannot saw it, chip it, shovel it or import it as fast as we will need to burn it! We were counting on the French starting without delay."

Toby could bear it no longer, he risked an unwise interruption of the minister's discourse, "Ma'am, forgive me but what has this to do with the North Koreans?"

"More than you will realise, Toby. If you'd *permit* me?" she said, her hazel eyes suddenly boring into the screen.

"Sorry, Ma'am."

A flicker of annoyance crossed her visage. Clearly the Minister was not used to and didn't take to being interrupted. In common with a lot of politicians, she certainly liked the sound of her own voice.

Toby looked back a little sheepishly but remained riveted to the screen, nevertheless.

"Sensing the embarrassment of HM Govt., we were approached by Rolls-Royce."

"The car manufacturer, ma'am?" said Toby, with mounting puzzlement.

"*No,* Mr Richmond," her eyes shot skywards with frustration, "and it might be best if you just listen for the moment."

"Sorry Ma'am," he repeated, defensively, but a little more loudly at this outing.

"We were approached by Rolls-Royce, the *aero*-engine manufacturer. As you may know they have held an interest in power generation using gas turbines for some time and have had many contracts around the world. You may also know that they manufacture and install nuclear plants, small ones, so called micro-generation power plants in nuclear submarines. The steam so generated is then used to propel and power the submarine without any emissions, which is so vital to a submarine's ability to stay submerged for months on end and to remain undetectable."

More questions and incredulity wracked Toby's brain mercilessly, but he knew that he'd better not interrupt the Minister again. He decided to remain patient and simply continued to nod, doing his best not to appear stupid.

"Rolls-Royce approached us and offered us a new slant on micro-generation. This is where multiple small nuclear plants, that are tried and tested and readily available and can be installed quickly, are chained together to run in parallel and, in so doing, feed directly into the National Grid. We thought this would save us. We were all set up to install a trial power plant based on this technology."

Toby nodded, with some relief. Finally he was making some inroads into the information that had been given to him.

"In an embarrassment of riches, at the same time we were then approached by Qinetiq, the multi-national defence contractor, based in Hampshire."

"You *were* ma'am?" said Toby sensing that there was more puzzlement to come.

The Minister paused; Toby was dying to ask more questions at this point, but something told him she would continue to view any more interruptions in a bad light. He bit his tongue and waited. Her icy gaze remained directed toward him; suddenly her eyes narrowed as she put him under intense scrutiny.

"What I am about to tell you is *very* sensitive and known only to a few. It seems, however, unless I am very much mistaken, that our North Korean friends are already aware of much of what I am about to convey and this is why the matter has suddenly become of the highest urgency.

Two brilliant scientists contacted us from the British Power Division, a part of Qinetiq. They informed us that they had finally made a break-through solving the problems of a Thorium reactor. You may know that all the developed nations have been pumping money into this research. The Chinese and Americans, in particular, have invested billions. Thorium produces power with no CO_2 emissions, like a nuclear reactor, but without the attendant dangers and embarrassment of nuclear waste that nobody wants and that since Chernobyl, Three-mile Island and the Fukushima plant in Japan that was hit by an earthquake and tidal wave, everyone is frightened of.

What's more, their research was so advanced that we are told that a working plant will come on stream within two years. Gas plants can be used to keep the Grid up and running until this comes on line. We will build more if the tests are favourable. We hid a test plant, or so we thought, in a place that we didn't think anyone would look. There is an old nuclear plant near Cemaes bay on Anglesey."

Toby now started nodding vigorously as if the penny had finally dropped in a very complex and convoluted mechanism.

"We have a Thorium plant all set to go live in the middle of Wylfa power station near Wylfa Head, Anglesey. We don't know how, but it seems that this is why the North Koreans are here, and your work has alerted us to their interest. We expect they are here to steal either information, drawings, blueprints, our scientists, or all of these things.

The North Koreans are in dire straits. They have poured their entire Gross Domestic Product into creating and testing nuclear-armed ballistic missiles to spite the Americans. In so doing, not only is the population starving but their whole infrastructure is creaking to a halt, including the handful of oil-powered powerplants that they still have working and hundreds more coal-fired ones that they can no longer either service or afford spare parts for. The Chinese are so fed up with the belligerent stance they take as regards the USA, and are themselves under such intense pressure from the Americans, that even their patience is wearing thin and we are told they are about to cut them adrift. This is why they want to steal our work. It's a ready-made solution and our breakthrough means it's deliverable and, when compared to old nuclear plants that have suddenly been made obsolete, inexpensive.

"You must understand that this cannot be allowed to happen. In a further twist..."

Toby fought against but failed to resist the urge to reach up and scratch his head which not only felt as if it was on fire but also was aching under the deluge of unexpected, yet crucial and restricted, information. He was not sure that he could cope with more revelations. She paused, sensing his discomfort, but quickly dismissed such a thing. "In a further twist, you may know that some years ago Qinetiq was floated on the London Stock Exchange. The Americans purchased a controlling interest. Technically they should have been made aware of, and given full access to, this power generation programme."

She coughed a little embarrassingly; Toby sensed what was to come next. "But HM Government took the view that it was of such national importance that it should be withheld from even them. Apparently many around the Cabinet table thought this would pay the Americans back for implementing the McMahon Act."

Toby had never heard of the McMahon Act but knew that he could not interrupt Dame Helen again. Moreover, he was still digesting the explosive nature of the revelations from the Minister. He stared now wide-eyed and this was made worse by a fiery tightness in his throat that came over him. It was almost as if he'd been given a glimpse into the future; granted prescient vision for those thirty seconds while he saw, now, what lay ahead for Horizon and what she was about to do to them; betray them all for her own self-interest. He couldn't help but remember the little curl that appeared on the edge of just one of her lips, one that he had recognised on many previous occasions, when she was about to throw someone under a bus.

"This, of course, means that HM Government cannot, under any circumstances, be seen to be intervening. We therefore need a third party to act as our agent, so to speak, to covertly protect the national interest.

I wonder, therefore, as your team is fully engaged with this, if we could prevail upon Horizon to continue? I must inform you that the secrets contained within Wylfa are so important that personal factors must be held as a secondary consideration."

"So, Ma'am, are you saying that my agents may be at risk and they must be considered *expendable*?" Politicians always had polite nice-sounding words to hide unpleasant and dangerous actions. Toby wanted her at least to clarify this in plain English. It was even worse than he'd anticipated; his

heart started thumping like an angry colt in his chest as he
realised that not only were they expected to do others' dirty
work, but they were also expected to lay down their lives, if
the situation demanded such.

"I am, Mr Richmond. I can only say that it is a long time
since Britain has had home grown technology like this that
will truly be a world beater if we can, for once, only keep our
secrets."

"Very well, Ma'am, I understand. May I be given twenty-
four hours to discuss it with my agents?"

"No, Mr Richmond, I am afraid I will need an answer this
evening. Contact me again tonight at whatever time suits you.
If for any reason Horizon cannot deal with this and I have to
mobilise our security and armed forces, I will have to do so
without delay." She now looked very irritated and the tone of
her following words reflected this. He wondered if it was her
inconvenience that she was trying to limit.

"Such rapid mobilisation cannot be done without drawing
further attention from other interested parties. Moreover, it
will lead to more suspicion being placed on this quiet corner
of the world, precisely why we chose it, so that we could bring
our technology on stream without anyone noticing. Perhaps it
was a vain hope, especially in light of what your careful
monitoring has revealed. We are hoping that the North
Koreans' habits of secrecy and isolation mean that they will
have shared their new-found knowledge with few others. Very
well, Mr Richmond, if you would be so good as to come back
to me as soon as you are able. If your organisation is
unwilling or unable to complete," once again an icy edge
found its way into her voice, "then, I shall have no alternative
but to invoke our national security services and hope that such
an event does not trigger further interest from our cousins
across the pond and our communist friends who seem to take
an unnatural interest in all that we do."

Chapter VIII

Dirty Little Secrets

An hour later Toby contacted Dame Helen. Events had brought about a change to the whole of Horizon; this was the first time they had taken on a mission in which the safety of their agents was to be subservient to the priorities of the mission. Nevertheless, the agents voted unanimously to accept the situation, having been told that the mission, begun in such low-key circumstances, had now developed into one of national importance.

"Ma'am, thank you for speaking with me again so late."

"Not at all, Mr Richmond. I am aware of how much pressure I am putting both you and your team under." she offered almost as an irrelevance.

"All the agents are prepared to continue with the mission and they realise that a positive outcome, while we operate without regard to our personal safety, is of utmost importance." The words stuck a little as he said them but, once spoken, he knew that they had done the right thing. In truth he realised, national priorities in abeyance, they could hardly have come to any other conclusion. Mobilising the MI5 and MI6 so late and on such a scale would always attract attention, especially from the Americans, and once such attention was focussed it would not be long before the secret was out and everyone knew. Moreover, by using Horizon, the Government could retain deniability if things went wrong. By such means, secrets could remain hidden for longer or even blamed on the mistaken actions of a private security force. Moreover, if difficult decisions were taken that might at best be questionable in law, if not downright illegal, then once again, the Government could deny everything. This was the thing about dirty little secrets; the Establishment of the day would always be looking, and have a need for, people with the resources and compliance to keep them well away from public gaze.

"Very well, Mr Richmond, I will send more details by courier tonight." She tried, but couldn't quite defeat the flicker of a greedy smile from appearing on her face, like a poker player who was about to outwit her opponent. "Please, of course, treat such information as highly secret, strictly on a need to know basis. You are to continue to follow the North Koreans, find out what their plans are and, it goes without saying, you are to protect national secrets. Security at the plant is very tight already. We have told the press that a crack was detected in one of the old nuclear reactor vessels that are in the process of being decommissioned, and we are engaged in immediate reparative work, which explains the high security and the procession of traffic journeying to the Wylfa head. We don't think our visitors will be able to infiltrate the plant itself, which means we need to know exactly what they do. Please remember, too, that you are to regard the North Koreans' lives as being expendable, which is another reason why we are hoping you can deal with this without any official involvement and thus without triggering an international incident. No knowledge of your actions will be admitted at any stage."

"I understand, Dame Helen, thank you," he managed to say without any bitterness creeping into his voice.

"Lastly, Mr Richmond, is there any news of Miss Clancy?"

"Yes, Ma'am, I saw her a few days ago. I am afraid she is not fit to return."

"That is a shame, Toby, as it seems that at times like these she will be sorely missed."

"I am afraid so, Ma'am. I can't help but agree with you."

"Very good then, goodnight Mr Richmond. Expect some more files and information, which will be conveyed to you tonight."

"Yes, Ma'am," he managed, before she terminated the link.

For some time he sat quietly at his laptop, deep in thought. If things were handled badly or somebody did something stupid, then the casualty rate could climb alarmingly on a mission like this. He did his best to fight thoughts of just one of his agents from appearing in that moment. Dame Helen had given Toby leave to reveal to the agents just a little more about the sensitive nature of the operation and its crucial importance to the country. It was good that the response was unanimous and positive. Notwithstanding this, he could only pass on sketchy details of the true nature of the mission to his agents, but they were not stupid; no doubt many had already guessed the importance of what they had uncovered and the fact that it was linked to something or *someone* to be found within this quiet backwater of the Principality.

He wondered then, just how he could limit Janet's exposure, as a hasty move, not an uncommon thing when analysing her methods, could trigger a bloodbath when the stakes were so high. He would do his best to assign her to the surveillance role rather than the team that intervened when the data breach was uncovered. This made things at least a little easier for him especially if agents were to be sacrificed, if need be, for the greater good. Agents, having been given more detailed briefings, were immediately despatched to monitor the two key scientists involved in the project and their every movement. Wylfa power station was also in receipt of a new team of cleaners, whose duty roster placed one or more of them in work round the clock. Such staff went in that very night.

Toby moved straight to the operations room. This was a good way of monitoring the Horizon agents and their deployment in order to keep the North Koreans under discreet surveillance. He noted the position of all the agents and most, as usual, had kept their position indicators active whether on duty or not.

He noticed, and increasingly of late, that Tim and Janet were to be found together even though both were on rest days. He knew that with the forthcoming storm it might be weeks before any of them would be able to stand down. A short time later a high security clearance courier arrived with detailed and sensitive information in a briefcase chained to his wrist. The links of the chain clanked together with every step that he took. Toby noted that he was armed, wore a bullet-proof tunic and agreed to hand over that material only after scanning Toby's retinas despite his having met him several times before!

Janet and Tim were in a fashionable steak restaurant in the centre of Manchester.

"So, Tim, what's all the black ops stuff about?"

"Need to know I suppose, Janet, but Toby just said that we were to continue to monitor the North Koreans, that we'd stumbled into the middle of something of national importance and that if we were to continue, then the safety of each and every one of us would be subservient to the needs of the mission. He also said we are now going to observe two nuclear scientists. Apparently he's put Brady and Tomkins on it tonight already."

"Holy fuck, has anything like this happened before?"

"Well, of course, I am not the one to ask but I believe not. Even at the time of the Russian assassins it was very much an operation to contain and remove them with the expectation that Horizon would repair and rebuild − which of course we've done. This has the feel of something very different. I'm also not aware that the agents' lives have ever been seen as being subservient to the mission, right from the start."

"So, who are these scientists?" Janet's tawny eyes homed in on her partner like an owl spotting a mouse crossing a field on a moonlit night.

"I'm not sure who they are, only that Toby said they were crucial to the mission and working on something of national importance. Mellor and Crisk, I think Toby said. No doubt he's given Brady more information."

Janet now started nodding but remained deep in thought as her mind tried to think of exactly who and what was involved. She had a habit of rubbing her left wrist, and the FitBit fitness device that was to be found there, when she was concentrating to the exclusion of all else – as now.

"So, how many steps have you done today?" Tim nodded, as he looked at the pink band that she wore all the time.

"I guess, if you count bonking you, then it must be at least 20,000."

"Does it have a setting for bonking?"

"Holy fuck, yes, this is a special one modified just for me!"

He laughed. At this point his steak was brought to the table and also her tuna salad.

She looked at the large plate, which contained, barely, the largest steak she'd ever seen.

"Jeez, Tim, I thought the Texans liked their steak, but I think that half a cow that you have there would put even one of theirs to shame. Good job I made you work for it this afternoon. And whoa, look at those *chips*. You are a chip lover, aren't you!"

Tim looked at his plate and was a little fazed at first but then remembered the old joke about how one eats an elephant – one bite at a time. They finished their meal uneventfully and both enjoyed their leisure time together with few further thoughts about the mission that remained ahead.

That night, however, he awoke from a deep but short sleep. He could not understand why he felt both troubled and agitated. This, or so he initially believed, had not been helped by the secure communication that was received by all the agents, clarifying in more detail the nature of the operation. At first Tim thought that it must be Janet's volcanic snoring that had summoned him to wakefulness, or perhaps the further information that had been revealed. However, he realised in that moment that it had nothing to do with either of these things but something that he'd not even registered at the time.

Having recalled it, he knew that it had overarching importance. Even more than this, he wondered if it was something so crucial that the whole organisation was now in the greatest of danger – furthermore, it had nothing to do with the North Koreans but to do with someone far more dangerous to himself and each and every one of the Horizon team, as well as their loved ones.

He shook his head as he sat up in bed, making a physical attempt to dismiss his black thoughts and reset them on a more positive, brighter pathway. It was the middle of the night and sometimes in the depth of darkness one's mind could deceive one into thinking thoughts that would not bear scrutiny in the light of day.

He had a feeling, however, and so it came to be, that the harsh morning light that appeared the following day would crystallise his thoughts and his suspicions even more brutally and he realised with both alarm and sadness that this was indeed the case.

CHAPTER IX

Flicker of Doubt

The following day Janet left very early in order to travel to North Wales. She had been rostered to take part in the on-going surveillance of the North Koreans. To this end, all the agents had been pulled from other missions as soon as they could be re-allocated and this included the reserve force. She started her Mustang ostentatiously at 5 am and she then gunned the engine mercilessly, no doubt waking all their neighbours. Happily, she kept her favourite trick of spinning the driving wheels, leaving clouds of smoke in the process and months of normal tyre wear on the road, to a minimum before she shot away.

Tim's rota had him joining the operation a little later in the week. His head continued to burn with even more questions that his poor night had managed to generate, and these in turn were fuelled by mounting worries that left him feeling nauseous. Although he had not been able to get back to sleep his wakefulness had at least brought to him a plan of action. He knew that he would know no peace until he had satisfied his doubts and obtained the answers to the relentless flow of questions coursing through his brain. He also knew where his answers lay – perhaps the only crumb of comfort.

He drove to Salford Quays and went down to the operations room. Worries exerted their weight upon him, and on his expression, as he offered an eye up to the camera lens so that the on-duty operator could see him. He entered the four-digit code and the reinforced steel door opened quickly with only a slight buzzing noise betraying its labours.

Ambient lighting in the bunker was kept to a minimum. This allowed the agent in charge to view the high-resolution screens in even more detail and also served to minimise distraction as a constant stream of messages and captured sound and signals were relayed directly. The control lights, touch screens, cameras and communications hardware blinked and glowed as they gave off a variety of visual and auditory signals, with beeps signifying their continued functioning or state of readiness. Fans whirred quietly, keeping the air fresh and the electronic equipment cool. They all took their part in making up the vast and detailed collective consciousness of a modern operations room.

"Tim, what are you doing here?" Jenkins asked, not being used to seeing Tim in the bunker. He continued to flick switches and operate rotary and sliding controls as he simultaneously communicated with agents at the heart of the mission, whilst others remained to be drafted in on a regular basis as others were stood down.

"Oh nothing much; I just need access to some of the monitors for an hour or so. I am looking for something. Something that I think may be important."

"Oh, oh, sounds as if you are a man on a mission." Jenkins offered light-heartedly, not yet picking up on Tim's worried appearance. He nodded towards the console and arranged for access clearance for his colleague. "Okay, take a seat; you can then sign in and I'd better let you get on with it."

Tim made himself a strong coffee, passed a similar one to Jenkins, and sat down in front of one of the large monitors. He hesitated, gave off a long sigh, and for a moment thought that others would think him very silly and most likely paranoid if he revealed even a hint of his thoughts. This state did not last long as he realised that, if he was correct, then the sooner he knew the better for all concerned. Under these circumstances people could start dying within hours. If, on the other hand, he was wrong, then nobody ever need know.

He brought on line the off-site server that contained their stored and archived material from previous operations. Sitting in the subdued lighting seemed to focus his mind and he soon accessed the surveillance files and images that pertained to a mission he remembered well. This had been his first outir.g as Chef de Mission and he had been responsible for capturing and scrutinising all the images he'd seen that night, now many months ago. He remembered the scene and those images very well. Nevertheless, he had a strong feeling that there was something, something else contained in the video files that he'd not spotted before – or much worse, that he'd seen and not registered. He'd spent his time, as had everyone else that winter's night, on trying to identify the bomber who'd gained access to the American Embassy. Perhaps it was forgivable if they'd all missed something that was even now in the process of destroying them all. If only Miss Clancy was here she would know what to do. Many of the images featured her, sporting that sensational dress. He couldn't help but notice how stunning she looked as she moved so gracefully yet stealthily across the room. He stared at the screen having frozen the image of that wonderful smile she used to reassure, to engage, to distract and disarm those around her; and, without doubt, whenever she looked at Toby. He shook his head to align his thoughts to the vast amount of material he'd have to sift through.

Two hours later Toby arrived. He was due to take over the Mission Surveillance role from Jenkins later that afternoon. He sat next to Tim and in front of the large wall-based monitors that were blinking with the position and status of all the agents. As was his way, he liked to check in a little early then get some lunch before relieving his fellow agent. His mood was light-hearted and relaxed; how quickly this would change.

"Tim, what are you doing here? I thought we had you joining the operation day after tomorrow." He thought that Tim had simply popped in for a mission update and to enquire after their progress, and Janet's in particular. "Are you after Janet? Look, you can see her position, looks like she's over the straits, maybe on the suspension bridge? No doubt she is following our North Korean friends." He pointed to the large screen, turned the thumbwheel to zoom in on the display that indicated the position of every active agent and a good many of the others. He then realised that Tim was looking elsewhere and that Tim's furrowed brow and very presence hinted at something much more serious. "What's that you are looking at? Is that not the American Embassy? My, your first one as mission controller – and how well you did. Why are you looking through it now?"

Many questions delivered quickly concealed his mounting worry.

"Toby, I can't really be sure. I just know that I will know it when I see it."

"Anything important, Tim? Anything I need to be aware of? Do you need help?" Toby did not need to read Tim's expression for his own apprehension to rise in tandem. He felt his throat drying and could sense his eyes staring at Tim a little more than politeness would sanction. Moreover, he could sense Tim adopting a guarded demeanour.

"I hope I'm wrong but I just need to make sure. It might well be nothing; it's too soon to say. I will know when I have been through all the files. I need to do this alone if that's okay? Forgive me, Toby, I need to concentrate if I am going to find what I think might be hidden here somewhere."

As was his tendency, Toby sought solace in confirming the obvious. "Well, there are a few hours' worth there and then, of course, we have the ones we hacked from the embassy secure feed." Ultimately, as more anxiety rose within he just had to ask, "Do you think there is something of importance here? Is there something I should be worried about?"

Tim had displayed all their surveillance footage including that from Clancy's neck-cam on four different screens, and his eyes continued to stare unto the point of aching as he looked at absolutely everything. Nimble fingers ran overlapping and multi-sourced images on the split screens and Tim's eyes darted from one to another as he feverishly looked for something that his worst fears had told him, somewhere in the night, must be there.

"I just can't be certain, but I need to look through *everything* if need be."

Sensing that he was distracting his younger colleague, and taking the hint, Toby decided to change tack. He patted Jenkins on the shoulder. "I'm just going to grab some lunch and I'll be back in an hour in order to take over, Jenkins."

"Righto then, Toby, see you soon," he looked at the clock. "Absolutely no hurry, you are very early as usual, so take your time." Jenkins laughed as he said the words; he knew his boss very well. Jenkins darted a worried look over to Tim on the adjacent station: a look that mirrored Toby's.

"Please keep me informed, Tim, phone me any time."

"Will do, Toby," Tim nodded but didn't take his eyes from the screens, "I am off to see my Mum and Dad as soon as I've done this but I'll be sure to let you know, and as soon as, if I find anything." Tim did his best to remove the concern from his voice, but Toby had long since guessed something of serious import was afoot.

It was to be about thirty minutes later that Tim found what he'd hoped he would not. He used the rotary control to slow and then to advance the video footage one frame at a time. He flicked it back and forth, hoping if he viewed it once more the dreadful image would somehow change or even disappear. Sadly, it was not to be; all he could do was stare at the malevolent image he'd captured as it continued to glow back with inerasable menace. He knew in this moment that his life had changed, as had everyone else's. For certain the mission was in jeopardy, which was the least of his concerns. Even more than this, and exactly as he feared, all the agents were now in the most extreme danger, a fact that extended way beyond the parameters of the mission. He realised, too, that not only were the agents' lives at risk of being forfeit but also, more than likely, those of their loved ones. This was the cruellest aspect of his new-found knowledge; nobody would be spared − not even the innocent.

He'd frozen the frame but the image had long since burned itself onto his retinas. He would remember that image until the day he died. It lay in front of him almost like a challenge that mocked him and a declaration that none of them would be spared. He dropped his head and used his free hand to rub the back of his head as the cold sweat of unexpurgated fear established itself.

"Are you all right, Tim?" asked Jenkins, sensing Tim's unease.

Tim could barely speak, "Yes thanks, I'm off," said Tim. "I'll be in touch later." He knew he had to get out of there as quickly as possible. He printed a couple of the frozen images but certainly didn't want to answer questions about what he'd been looking for. Sickness welled up from within. He flicked the button to clear the contents of the screen just as Jenkins' turned to look in his direction.

"Oh okay, Tim," concern now creeping into his voice, which mirrored his young colleague's.

This was the worst thing about Tim's discovery; he was not sure who to trust with the knowledge that he'd uncovered. He knew that he had to run, to escape, and hope to clear his head; most of all he needed time to think. What was even worse, he now knew that it was his fault. He'd brought this upon not just himself but everyone else, too. How could he have been so blind not to see what was now all too apparent? It was this, abject shame, that dictated that he run from the scene as quickly as possible until he had time to clear his head and decide what to do.

He found his car in the secure car park. He did not remember making the drive to Alderley Edge, arriving there early evening. Janet phoned him as he was driving.

"Where are you lover; had a real aching for you tonight. Nearly shot two of these Korean bastards just to keep myself occupied. I am bored out of my tree."

"Oh, don't do that, Janet, or we'll never know what they are really up to."

"Only joking, lover, where are you?"

"Oh, just popping over to see my Mum and Dad."

"Jeez," she said a little deflatedly. "Well, I'll see you in a day or two?"

"You sure will," he said, aping her American accent.

He went into the house quietly. He was not surprised to find his parents waiting for him, sitting in the kitchen. They liked to make something of an occasion each and every time he ventured home. They both rushed to their feet as he came in. Margaret insisted on making him a cup of tea and then something to eat. All the staff had gone home but she liked it best on such occasions as it gave her a chance to fuss over her son and only living child.

"No Janet, Tim?" Margaret asked a little cautiously, but nodded as she saw her hopes rewarded.

"No, Mum, she's on stakeout, I'll be meeting up with her later in the week."

Margaret couldn't hide her delight at the words. For a day or two at least she'd have her son to herself and she'd be able to quiz him about all the things bubbling through her active mind. She began by asking him about his work as much as she thought polite and did her best not to pry as to confidential events. Inevitably, whether he was alone or otherwise, she found herself unable to ask about the one person she wanted to ask him about more than any other: the second person who was now absent from all their lives.

He knew that his Mum didn't care for Janet; she never had and never would. Moreover, the feeling was mutual. His Dad, in one of his more philosophical moments, had informed his son that, as regards his choice of partner, it had to be his choice to make and, having done so, he could be sure that both of them, including his Mum, would accept it with good grace. Until such time he must forgive his mother for continuing to hold out for another. Tim could see his Mum continuing to burn with doubts about Janet. Mercifully, Arthur was on hand to provide distraction and also to keep the conversation going without straying to the subject and the person that Margaret craved to discuss above everything and *everyone* else.

That evening, however, something even more pressing stirred in the unspoken gaps between their words and both parents could tell that their son was not only deep in thought, but also troubled. They sat with him while he ate his food. This only served to increase his nervousness. He toyed with the jacket potato as if it reminded him of something very painful. None of this was lost on either his Mum or Dad.

After some time Arthur made coffee for Tim and tea for himself and his wife.

"Mariah has made your room up, Tim. We weren't sure if Janet would be coming with you, so there are two lots of towels and so on."

"Thanks, Mum."

Margaret made some small talk about Janet and how pleased they were to see him. That evening, however, she swiftly moved the conversation on. He sipped his coffee more precisely than ever and he seemed content to stare into its steaming, glossy surface rather than to look up at either of them. Some mums would call it intuition; others the invisible umbilical cord, and many more would just call it perceptiveness. In any event, whatever it was called, it was in full force now. Eventually her words precipitated like rain falling from a cloud.

"Tim, what is it, what's troubling you?" The illimitable blue of her eyes met his with unwavering concern.

He nearly made the mistake of attempting the lie, but he knew that she would detect this at first offing; such was the scrutiny she'd placed him under.

"We've got trouble." He shook his head at the inadequacy of his words; thereby immediately damaging his attempt to reassure her.

"Trouble?"

"What sort of *trouble*?"

He knew then that attempting to limit or fudge his answers to her would be destined to fail even as they left his mouth.

"We, *all* the agents are in danger. The whole of Horizon, and I expect it will extend to all our loved ones too –

everyone. Horizon's security has been compromised. I am not sure how deep it runs but it's at the highest level. I don't know who I can tell, because it's all my fault. I am really frightened. I've seen on countless occasions how these people operate. They shoot first and ask questions later. Nobody will be spared once they sense what is out there and what we've tried to hide."

"But I thought the whole thing had been revised, safeguards put in place to protect the agents," the sound of desperation rising in the tone of her voice.

"Yes we did, we looked at the whole thing before Miss Clancy left. But this, this danger extends way past that. Whatever resources we can bring into play won't be enough. There'll never be enough, not with these people, and it may already be too late."

"Who can you tell, who can you trust?" His mum's voice was unusually loud as she reflected the panic she could see rising in her son, made worse by the number of questions that queued in her restless brain.

"I am just not sure."

"Well I am, Tim. There's one person you can definitely tell and that is Toby. What have you said to him?" She was calmer, at least for the moment, as some order in the chaos was restored to her.

"Yes, I can trust him, but can one man save us all?"

"Well, I don't know," she offered, the desperation creeping ever further into her voice, "But I *do* know he is a good place to start, so phone him tonight, phone him *now*."

Before he did so Tim clarified the specific nature of his concerns.

They both listened with wide-eyed incredulity at how the organisation could have been compromised, so quickly and so comprehensively.

"Tim, you are correct, I fear none of you are safe; you must tell Toby immediately; phone him," advised his father, his voice now shaking. "Another thing, son, this is in no way your fault. You cannot be held to account for *this*. I'm certain Toby will agree with me."

"Can you pull out of your current mission?" asked Margaret.

"No, we are in too deep. Pulling out will raise more suspicion and they will be on us even sooner. If they detect we are pulling out they'll assume we have what they want and they will kill us all just to get it." He swallowed hard, desperately trying to calm the panic that had overrun him and been made that much worse by his telling them. "Our only chance is to go forward with it as if we are in blissful ignorance and hope that when the time comes, *if* the time comes, we can save ourselves. It's not just us; *you*," he almost shouted the word and then came a pause as he re-aligned his thoughts, calming himself a little, before continuing, "and lots of loved ones will be targets too; that's how these people work. Their reputation for brutality is well known."

"Cancel the mission, Tim, pull out if you have to and come and stay with us," was the only thing that a mother could say.

"Mum, *listen*; it's gone too far for that; we won't be *safe* here and neither will you. *They* can always find us, that's what they do *and* they will, wherever we try to hide. This is what they do and they are good at it; they will exploit any weak areas, find loved ones and drag them into danger. Then they strike; nothing is beyond these people, especially when the stakes are as high as now. I have to go forward, pretend there's nothing wrong and hope that when the time comes it isn't too late to act. At that time, I will save as many as I can."

Her mind still in a whirl, Margaret asked what she'd been meaning to ask for some little while. "But *how* did you uncover it? How did you work out all this!"

Tim laughed; Arthur wondered if his son was hysterical. "As always, something simple, something easy to miss, but once I'd picked up on it I just knew. I knew I had to follow it and once I'd done so, I could see that it leads right back to all of us." He told them of his discovery that had been present in the surveillance tapes ever since their mission in the American embassy. Arthur couldn't believe what he'd just heard.

"Tim, I am so sorry it's come to all this," said Arthur. "Is there time for us to get out, to travel perhaps?"

"No, Dad they'd find us *wherever* we are; we have to keep the force together and act when we can. It's the only way; at least we are forewarned and so are you."

Just before she spoke, Arthur detected the slightest flicker of delight on his wife's face accompanied by the briefest of glances in his direction. It was all too briefly and rapidly subsumed by her worry but he knew then what her next words would be.

Margaret spoke as silence and deep thought fell between them. She mentioned the person who'd been constantly in her thoughts. The words appeared with such moment, it was like a dam bursting. "We thought we'd get used to seeing you in danger; that you'd always be able to keep yourself safe." Given what she'd just heard it seemed entirely appropriate that she mentioned the name of the person who was never far from her mind. "You *and* Miss Clancy; she was your talisman, there to protect you, somehow. And now she's gone." The pause itself added resonance to her words: they were the words that she'd promised herself that she would not say and here, at the eleventh hour, she knew she could no longer stop herself. "But *this,* Tim, this is too much. Is there *anything* we can do?"

"Yes, Mum, we have to hold on and hope we can all get through this."

"Tim, *go* and phone Toby, call from the other room. The sooner he knows the better," concluded his father as he pointed to the quiet that was to be found in his study.

Tim picked up his Blackberry, which he'd retrieved this from his agent's pack and which was part of their 'Mission Compromised Protocol'. These older devices still ran the secure messaging service on secure servers and conveyed messages that could not be hacked. Having switched on the device, he phoned Toby. Moreover, confidential messages could be sent to specific agents without any danger of eavesdropping.

Toby listened to the news with incredulity.

"Oh, Tim, this is bad, really bad. I knew it must be bad when the Blackberry went off. I just knew you were on to something in the bunker. I could tell then it was serious. We are in this right up to our necks now: we can't pull out and yet, if we stay in, we'll be obliterated." Toby thought aloud feverishly.

"*She* had a feeling about this. She *knew* it was heading south and she let us take it on, so she didn't have to get her *own* hands dirty or have difficult conversations with her superiors."

Although neither was Tim party to confidential communications, nor was Dame Helen's name mentioned, he did not have to think too hard to guess whom Toby was thinking about. "Our only hope is the advantage of surprise. We need to be very careful. The other thing I need you to do is to continue to communicate by Blackberry and only with those we know we can trust. Remember that our digital comms device can be picked up and monitored by absolutely everyone. It's good that you've brought this to me now, Tim, and at least we won't go down without a fight, I promise. Please leave it with me. I'll be in touch soon."

"I am sorry about this, Toby, I know it's all my fault."

Toby laughed, all too briefly, "*No,* Tim, it's not your fault. If anything you have given us a chance or we'd all be toast, shot in the back, or each of us would have met with accidents that would be hushed up and our sacrifice would never have come to the light of day, while various governments glossed over it all; somehow patched it all up before we were cold in the ground. Well, it ain't going to happen, not while I'm still breathing. I'll be in touch later; get some sleep while you can. Please don't blame yourself, I need you thinking clearly because only then will you give of your best and that is what we are all going to need to be, *at our very best,* if we are to come through this. I think you've done remarkably well to uncover it with what you had to go on. So many would have ignored what you picked up on. Well done, Tim."

Toby put the phone down. He knew that he now faced his greatest ever personal danger, up an order of magnitude, if not more, from the time when the Russian assassins were charged with liquidating them all. At that time there were simply two of them with limited resources. Now ranged against them was an entire organisation with limitless capability. In committing all of Horizon's agents in order to carry out what had seemed like a simple but painstaking surveillance operation, he'd unwittingly exposed them to a force who had the cunning, the resources and wherewithal to annihilate them all. Moreover, they would spare nobody and would kill without hesitation. Most significantly, their callous and single-minded determination to secure their objective while the body count rose would not only be forgiven but would be rewarded by their masters, while the British Government looked the other way, just as it always did under such a stand off. And the incident, just like his entire force, would be quietly forgotten before the ink was dry on the deals that would be done; all under the auspices of better relations between nations and co-operation between governments.

He refused to go quietly to his death without at least informing his contact as to what he now knew. Toby invoked the secure communication link on his laptop. The machine warbled a little as it paged this person. Dame Helen appeared on screen after a longer delay than usual. Toby had looked at the time but realised that what he had to say would wait not a minute longer. She looked a little dishevelled, sitting there in her bath robe, but had already guessed that the information he had to impart was of monumental significance. However, being the consummate politician, below which lay all other priorities, including the relative unimportance of his life and that of everyone he'd ever cared about, she almost successfully hid her alarm and anxiety below a dispassionate and clinical air. She told him that his organisation had offered to take it on. It was far too late for her to implement another strategy and, in an incautious moment, hinted that it would be her political suicide if she did so. She then informed him that his country requested and required of him that he do his duty. He knew the risks beforehand and he knew now precisely what was at stake. It was unfortunate that he faced such an efficient and ruthless foe but this, without doubt, was the environment that he'd chosen to work in, in both good and bad times. Surely she did not need to remind him of what he must do. What applied to him also applied to the rest of his team.

Toby in turn declared that he had no intention of backing out; that they would see things through to either a successful conclusion or the demise of the whole force if the situation required; that he was informing her only as a matter of courtesy.

She thanked him cordially, but the icy veneer that all politicians espoused at such times, meaning that he was expendable and she was insulated, whatever happened, was very much in evidence. Just before she terminated the link she offered, almost as an afterthought, to discuss things with her team the following day and see if any assistance could be provided, though such help, if any, would be limited to a strict background role and in no circumstances was this to be overt in any sense of that word. Her distraction as she spoke the words conveyed all that he needed to know; little help, if any, would be made available to them.

Toby stared at the blank screen for some time. His own grave image reflected in its funereal blackness just as hers had departed into a much brighter backdrop.

Meanwhile, having spoken to Toby, Tim went to find his mum and Dad.

"I've informed Toby, he will let me have his response in an hour or so."

"Look, you two, it's late; why don't you get some sleep?" Margaret suggested to the two men.

"I just have the kitchen to tidy and then, Arthur, I'll be up to bed." Arthur could at first see no logic in this. "Margaret, surely Mariah will do that in the morning. We have to give the poor girl something to do."

"Now, Arthur, you know how I hate going to bed with an untidy kitchen. Besides, that young woman does *quite* enough for us already."

Arthur sighed a little but he knew that this was his wife's way and there would be no changing her after so many years. He went out of the kitchen and up to bed.

CHAPTER X

Safe Harbour

Toby sat for a little while in the gathering darkness. Inevitably his thoughts drifted to his friend, Clancy. His mind turned back to the day he first saw her. At the age of thirteen she'd petitioned the court to be allowed to live on her own. Toby and his legal team were finalising the estate owing to his having just lost his entire family, at the age of eighteen. He was coming out of court as she was going in. Any feelings of self-pity were swept away instantly by one look at the emaciated and deeply unhappy young woman who was clearly going through purgatory; and this was some time before he'd learnt the entirety of her suffering at the hands of her foster parents. Something told him that he had to act and that it had to be soon. Things became even more pressing when her application was thrown out and her care was to remain with social services and with Roy. She looked as if she were in total despair.

He introduced himself to her and with no further delay asked her if he could petition the court so that she could be made his ward, under supervision from the court and social services, until she reached eighteen. He remembered that she'd said nothing but a little nod appeared, amidst a fixed expression of mistrust and fear, having decided that she could not remain where she was for another night. He instructed his legal team to make the application immediately and though it was hotly contested by social services Toby won through with the proviso that social services retained overall supervision.

Although some dreadful times lay ahead, it non the less represented a new beginning for both of them and neither would ever look back. Moreover, she, too, was alone in a world in which there was not another living soul who cared whether she lived or died.

He remembered the time that she had thanked him for giving her a home, a safe haven, and for allowing her to rebuild her life. With his help, and under his guidance, she'd accomplished so many things that otherwise she would have never dared to contemplate, let alone accomplish. All he'd had to do was provide a little stability, a safe harbour and an opportunity to try out for whatever star she felt she could reach. And she'd reached so many: so many that he'd become bewildered and awestruck in equal measure just bearing witness. Her life had been transformed and had contained so many exciting and worthwhile vistas yet, catastrophically, this had only brought into focus the one thing that it lacked.

Even more than this, he should have known that Clancy's desire to face her deepest fear and greatest tormentor would destroy her, to such an extent that her only recourse would be to exit and now, it appeared, never to return. If only he'd known sooner. If only he'd talked her out of it. He reasoned, however, on more reflection that he could do no such thing; this was her way of resolving things, something that she'd done and albeit paid a high price for. Even if by some means he could go back in time and be with her while she determined to put that last act in place, he could not contemplate attempting to dissuade her, nor would he ever wish to do so.

Ultimately this was his secret, the thing that he should have told her before she left, that she, by her very presence and daily example, had brought out qualities in him that she always said were lacking in herself. He knew now that he'd have to summon each and every one of these attributes if they were to stand a chance of coming through this. Most importantly, not unlike Clancy, he was at his best when the situation seemed dire and the odds of success were stacked against him. It was just one of the many things that bound them together. He invoked such qualities in that moment.

The large monitor on his wall flickered into life. Using his bespoke planning software he ranged all the agents along one side and then created a timetable of the events that would unfold as he saw it. To each of these likely events, and most of the unforeseen ones that he could only imagine, he assigned an agent. He soon ran out of personnel to cover each slot. This could only mean that they would have to work, as he would, round the clock until they had evaded their pursuers or they had all been erased. He foresaw too that his detailed plans were only the start; so many possibilities may yet come to pass that he would have to be ready to tear the whole thing up if need be and start again.

Under the auspices of the 'Mission Compromised Protocol' he contacted each and every one of his agents and gave them new instructions. Working feverishly through the night he drew up detailed plans, which he passed to them all. He also gave them instructions, much beloved by Clancy herself, of what to do under each of the possible scenarios that they were likely to face and, especially, what to do if things went wrong.

Margaret looked at the kitchen drawer for some time. Tim had told her there was only one person he could trust, but she knew of one other. As soon as both men had gone to bed, she opened the drawer furtively, even though she was now quite alone.

If she hesitated at all it would have been imperceptible to all but the keenest observer. If there was one thing in her life of which she was sure, this was it.

Just before she acted, however, Arthur came into the kitchen. Initially he had heard some of the clattering as his wife had tidied the kitchen, then all had gone quiet. A single moment of clarity had come to him, in that second, as he was changing for bed and with it came the knowledge of what his wife was about to do. He'd hurried downstairs.

"I thought you'd gone to bed, my love?"

"Margaret, I know you! We've not been together for all these years for me not to know, I could tell you were up to something and suddenly it came to me." He nodded at the device that Margaret held in her hand like a key to the vault of all knowledge.

"Are you sure, my love, it's been some time. What if she's forgotten us?"

His wife's initial reply was a simple exclamation, "Ha!" Then with more finality, "That'll never happen. No offence, Arthur, but I've never been more sure of anything in my whole life."

His eyes lit up as he nodded. At that moment both realised that not only were they of the same mind, but also somehow they were closer to Miss Clancy. Her eyes glowed like twin diamonds that had been tinted by pure Boron, with the effect of creating the palest of blue colours that glistened as the tears welled from within.

"Then press it, my love." He swallowed hard against a dry throat.

The mobile device glowed with comforting hues as she held it. She pressed it and the glow flared brighter, almost with an urgency, as if summoning a charm from an ancient amulet, that had been buried for centuries until the time came to awaken the forces within. The screen glowed for a second or two longer and then a graphic of a microphone appeared on the screen now black with the words 'Record your message'.

Margaret had clearly rehearsed what she was going to say. She lifted the device so as to bring it nearer to her mouth and began to speak. Even her prepared message, however, could not filter out her pleading tones despite the considerable effort she made to do so.

"Penny, please forgive me, but you said we could use this to contact you. They are in trouble; something's gone terribly wrong. Tim, Toby, *all of them*, are in danger. Tim says they've invoked the 'Mission Compromised Policy', or something. They face overwhelming odds and they've been told they are all expendable. The Government are selling them all down the river. Help us Penny, I'm begging you. SOS. Only *you* can save them. *They* need you." Only at this point did her voice falter… "and so do we." Another delay in her speech was accompanied by tears that began their noiseless but unceasing procession down both cheeks; the soft wrinkles and laughter lines diverting their progress. "Without you all will be lost, I just know it. We *can't* lose another, Penny. Forgive me, I know you wanted to wash your hands of all this but there's nowhere else to turn. You are our only hope. Save him Penny, I *beg* you. We don't matter so much, we've had our lives," she gripped Arthur's hand as she said this and continued, "but save *him* Penny, you are our only hope and his, too. Do this for me, my love, if you can." She released the virtual button on the touch screen. The microphone disappeared at this and formed an image of a silver envelope which glowed for less than a second and began to spin as it faded into the depths of the screen. Margaret hastily wiped her eyes. Arthur moved to squeeze her shoulder as he comforted his distraught wife; new words appeared on the device. "Your voicemail is in progress."

Having worked through almost all of the night, Toby was exhausted. He was too tired to find his bed and simply collapsed on the sofa. Lastly, just before he managed to grab an hour's, much needed, sleep he contacted Captain Richards on the *Ma Puissance.* He knew that they'd undergone an engine refit at a yard in Trieste. He held his breath while he asked the Captain if they were seaworthy. In an unusual request he was planning to ask them to leave immediately and make for Cavtat near Dubrovnik.

"Bill, it's Toby here, sorry to trouble you so late. I'm praying that the engine refit is complete. How soon can you set sail?" Something of Toby's grave expression conveyed instantly that apologies were the last things needed. "It's all gone pear-shaped here. I'd like you to weigh anchor this evening," he paused as he looked at the clock, "sorry I mean this morning, or just as soon as you are able. I'd like you to issue guns to all the crew and as you'll have a little time please get them up to speed with target practice as soon as you are able as I know many of them will be rusty."

"Oh yes, Toby, something bad in the offing? We should be signed off as soon as the yard opens. They usually like to do a quick sea trial, but I'll ask them to dispense with this at our risk, if that's okay? I take it we are the last refuge if things head south?" Captain Richards and Toby had gone over this scenario many times in the past. They'd had what seemed now like a low-key rehearsal when the Russians were at large but the Captain realised from the outset that this was far more serious for each and every one of them. Moreover, he could tell without his boss confirming it to be so who was after them, by witnessing the sheer horror on his face. He realised it really couldn't be anyone else.

Toby's eyes looked leaden and sore as he stared, having little energy left for anything other than talk. "Yes, Bill, I am afraid I'll need you somewhere where we can get to you by air quickly and at short notice. Cavtat harbour seems the best choice. I know it's quite a way south for you and I'd like you there as soon as you can. Please overrun the engines for as long as the engineer will tolerate. Run them at 110% if you are able but I need you at Cavtat as soon as. I will notify you when our charter is in the air and you should prepare to receive passengers, I am afraid there will be quite a few and it's no exaggeration to say that if you have to, then string hammocks from the bulkheads and make use of all the available space. You'll also need to lay-in ample provisions. It may be that you'll come under attack, so don't take any chances. You'll be most vulnerable while you are at anchor so please post sentries. As soon as you have your passengers then make for the open seas and be suspicious of anyone who approaches. If need be, get the crew to man the sides. I'll only be able to spare Monty to act as escort, so your crew will have to provide close protection duties."

"Whoosh Toby, sounds as though you have your hands full there."

"A bit of an understatement, in truth, Bill. It may well be that you will sail through unmolested but please do not assume that; do not let your guard down at any time. Be very suspicious, even the most innocent-looking pleasure boat that pulls up alongside may represent a danger to you. I will send you more information by secure link as soon as I am able. For now go and sweet talk your engineer and get those engines running as soon as."

"Righto, Toby, you look dreadful, get some sleep. Please don't worry about us, seems as if you have enough on your plate. I'll be on my toes, I promise, and I think a little shooting practice for the crew will shake them up a bit. Also, it's about time we gave those engines some work to do."

There was a pause and some movement from his lips before Toby eventually found the words. "I'll be sending confidential files with Alexis, you'll be the most senior if things go badly here, so feel free to read those articles and act accordingly."

It was now the turn of Captain Richards to pause, his hazel-green eyes stared at the screen as he did his best to digest new information that he'd not encountered before. He realised in that moment that Toby was indeed planning on a potential fight to the death for all active agents. Ultimately, he sought refuge in doing his duty by his friend and colleague. "Yes, of course, Toby, rest assured I will protect that information and do whatever is required to protect the crew and passengers. You have my word."

Toby nodded; he wasn't sure if exhaustion was about to claim him or emotion. In either case it was time to let the *Puissance* get underway. A weak smile followed the nod and Toby terminated the link with a dab of his index finger.

The thought that came to him just before he lapsed into a sleep, accompanied by much frightening imagery, was that he would do everything in his power to save as many of his agents as possible and also deny their adversaries their prize. He just hoped that it wasn't too late.

CHAPTER XI

Death By Drink

At this time darkness covered Clancy almost totally. There were occasional hints of a new day peeping through gaps in the closed shutters on the outside of her cabin but for some time she had neither been able, nor bothered, to venture out in order to open them. Any such trips beyond her cabin were confined simply to secure more supplies of gin. It had long since supplanted the need for food. In a strange but grisly reality, she recognised that darkness had occupied her life since the day her parents had been ripped away in the train crash that then consumed them violently and indiscriminately. It was at that time that the lights had gone out and she knew now that they'd never come back on. She'd waited, a terrified teenager of thirteen, being unable to get out of the washroom until the rescue teams had cut her out.

Her entire life had, from that point on, skirted round the dark like an unpowered satellite neither able to defy gravity, nor able to rotate towards the sun. If only she'd been sitting with them, then she could at least have the satisfaction of being with them and accompanying them, wherever that might be. Oblivion was better than this. At first, alcohol promised to insulate her from the horrors that existed in the darkness and then it offered a way of removing her from it completely. All she had to do was to continue to drink. She grasped at the bargain without a second thought.

The message traversed the world in rather less time than Margaret had taken to compose it. Clancy was about to pour herself another drink when she heard the device 'ping' on the other side of the room, where she'd left it. The second thing she noticed just as it gave off its insistent tone was that it started glowing in the darkness. She looked at her right hand as if it were no longer part of her: its trembling certainly now well beyond her control. Moreover, she'd been drifting in and out of consciousness for a day or two. She was no longer aware of day, date or time; such things had long since become an irrelevance. Although she wasn't aware of it, her skin had taken on a slight yellow hue. Nor had she noticed that her palms had become bright pink: the so-called 'liver palms' by the medical profession. She did know, however, that the best way of stopping the shaking was to drink more gin. Clancy had never seen the old T-shirt with the cruel joke on it. "Avoid hangovers – Stay drunk"

Had she seen it, she would know that this canard was very much in force. Drinkers felt so dreadful when making an attempt even to cut back that, very soon, the effort was beyond them, as was now the case for her. She could barely rise from the sofa that she'd been lying on for some days, let alone walk across the room to collect the device that now hummed insistently. Eventually, after some false starts, she staggered towards the device that continued to glow. Her head pulsated as a headache appeared that insisted that, if she'd just have another drink, then she'd feel so much better.

Rather than reach for another bottle, however, she approached the shelf, after much stumbling in the dark interior, on which lay her mobile device. The screen glowed with a silver envelope and the words, "New message received – Wainwright device." By using her left hand, which trembled a little less than her right, she was able to touch the envelope and the device then began to give up its message.

She saw the bottle of gin with its open top. It would be so much easier if she were only to lift it to her lips and drink freely. Surely, this was a quicker way of getting the life-giving liquid inside her – what did it matter if it was also killing her? Somewhere deep within as she heard Margaret's voice, a modicum of logic prevailed that had not yet been swamped by alcohol's all-pervading takeover of her mind and her body.

She remembered, somehow, that Margaret was neither one to panic nor to exaggerate. Clancy then heard the pleading tones and a little spark was kindled somewhere in the deepest, longest and deadliest of nights. She remembered, too, a promise, one that had been freely given and one that could not now be retracted. Once again, using her left hand to support the right, she succeeded in resolutely screwing the top back on the gin bottle. This alone took her an age, but somehow once it was done it remained as a talisman to draw her from a purgatory that alcohol had taken her to, yet paradoxically numbed her from.

A little while later, after drifting back from an unnatural doze, she managed to fill her glass with some ice and water, most of which covered the floor. By supreme effort using both hands she managed to raise this to her lips and a little of what remained within hit her lips. The water in turn started to burn her stomach that had long since grown accustomed to neat gin. She did her best to capture a little of the fluid and prevent at least some of it from spilling down her front. Emboldened by the most simple of successes in imbibing a few sips of water, she sought to try a little more. Before she did so, however, she composed a reply to Margaret. After several attempts she was able to activate the 'respond' button and recorded her message before facing similar problems in pressing 'send' that waited patiently on screen. It comprised "Message received, Margaret, and understood. I'll do my best to save him and as many others as I can, love Penny."

After sipping a little more water she must have passed out again. Prior to this, in a moment of insight, she wondered if she was still physically capable of travelling and if so how long a journey might take her. She awoke after about another hour and experienced severe tremors, which were uncontrollable: this timeframe being a long period for her to go without alcohol. She might have known, but had long since stopped caring, that it was a physical as well as psychological dependence and now as its malign force hit her, her body knew it too. Somehow, by dint of mercy of mercies her brain was spared the common fate that befell alcoholics who dared to frustrate the steady stream of the alcohol intake – the withdrawal fit that could be long, recurrent and deadly. She tried some more water but, in a further warning from the alcohol that sought to punish her for even thinking of making an attempt to break free, she was initially uncontrollably sick, before she collapsed on her knees. Some time later she managed to get back on her feet and even succeeded in filling a canteen with water and tried to venture outside.

In the early hours of the morning Margaret and Arthur, who had both stayed up, received her message. They thought that the slurring in her speech was due to distortion from the device and, otherwise being in blissful ignorance as to her true state, they both tried to get a couple of hours sleep. Margaret couldn't help but wonder if they had just invited the young woman back to face her own death. More than this, not that they were to know, there were doubts as to whether Clancy was able to save herself, let alone anyone else.

As Toby slept all the agents were already converging on Anglesey. This was not the only place where battle would be joined. Every agent, their families, their loved ones; even their relatives might be placed under threat at any moment. Toby had drawn up a list of those he had the resources to protect. Sadly, the cut-off line seemed much nearer the top than he'd have liked. If it hadn't come to him in his fitful dreams, then the thought certainly would be a recurring one in the days ahead – just how many of them would still be alive at the conclusion of this mission?

CHAPTER XII

Helping Hand

Toby dragged himself off the sofa feeling dreadful. His sleep had brought him very little by way of rest relaxation or recuperation. He went into his kitchen in search of a cup of strong coffee, which at least provided some warmth while the automatic movements allowed him to collect his thoughts. He knew there was still much to do. In some ways directing his agents was the easy bit. Both he and they would benefit from being kept busy and he had devised a tightly-packed rota, which provided for each of them, and also for himself, little opportunity to relax. Toby knew that the most difficult parts of his plans were still to come and the one conversation that he dreaded the most was the one with Alexis who would insist on knowing more than he could tell her. And yet he needed her co-operation if he was to save her and many of the others.

Having finished his coffee he chased a few crisp, then increasingly soggy, cornflakes round a bowl containing cold milk. He was almost relieved when his laptop began humming with the arrival of a secure call.

Dame Helen at least looked as if she'd had a good night's sleep. Her bath robe was now replaced with a more typical suit that she usually sported.

"Good Morning, Mr Richmond," she paused a little as she took in something of his appearance but then continued. "I have briefed some of my staff and I do have some good news for you. It seems that the main communication link from Anglesey to the mainland has been severed by a catastrophic fire at the central exchange. This means that there are no landline calls or internet calls available on the whole island. It seems somewhat coincidentally," she paused again so that he could take up her hidden meaning, "that several of the key mobile telecoms masts are closed for urgent repairs. You can appreciate how unlucky the islanders are with no Internet, no fixed-line telecoms and also no mobile signal across the whole island. I'm sure there'll be hell to pay.

HM Govt is also testing a new Army attack helicopter out of RAF Valley and in so doing we have had to insist that there be no direct flights either to, from or indeed *over* the whole island. It's a rare thing indeed that we close airspace in this way but we cannot have innocent people being exposed to danger while we do our tests." There was a mischievous glimmer in her eyes that he'd never noticed before as she continued. "As you might expect, we are working hard to stop the whole island from being cut off and we anticipate that we should have things up and running within two or three days, maybe four at the absolute most." She nodded slowly as she said these last few words so that he understood this was all the time she could give him. "Just to make sure that people are kept safe we have positioned a large contingent of police on both road and rail bridges from the island. I wonder if such unprecedented events might be used to your advantage? In what I am sure is another complete coincidence," once again her tiny eyes glimmered back at him for the briefest interval, "I am told that the Navy will be mounting extra patrols in the Irish Sea and these are sailing out of Liverpool as I speak." Toby's depleted state meant that he was unable to hide the incredulity that appeared on his face. Mercifully his dreadful appearance and her penchant, as with most politicians, for going on long and loud, meant she failed to detect it as she continued, barely pausing for breath, "They will take up station by the end of today. They are purely on a training exercise, which involves the part they would be asked to play if Britain were ever attacked from the sea. They will be in a constant state of high alert during these manoeuvres, which are due to last for a few days before they are stood down. I'm sure we've not seen anything like it since the Atlantic convoys of World War two. Not that I remember that, of course, she offered redundantly, or so she hoped. During this time I will be provided with regular updates from them and if there is anything at all that might be of interest to you, then I will be pleased to make it available to your organisation."

At a stroke, although not intervening directly, Dame Helen had provided essential support for the Horizon team and, at the same time, had made their job much easier, whilst making that of their adversaries much harder. Furthermore, as part of this, the removal and transmission of state secrets was now almost impossible without such information being physically carried off the island.

"Thank you, thank you, Dame Helen, such *unfortunate* events will indeed give us the advantage, especially over the North Koreans as they will be unlikely to have specialist satellite communication equipment with them. Of course, our main adversary will only be slowed a little by these measures and they will have access to a wealth of equipment, as you will know, at short notice. However, with the benefit of surprise I am hoping to stay ahead of them.

Thank you for your assistance Ma'am."

Toby was convinced that before she terminated the link with a perfunctory swipe of her hand he saw a tiny flicker of a smile, accompanied by some regret at the fate that she had selected them for. It was unlike her to show any emotion whatsoever. He shuddered a little as the look that she'd given off generated thoughts of a similar look being witnessed by those destined for the hangman's noose the following day from their captor. Hopefully, however, he could yet stay one step ahead and he went back to his plans, which were sent out to the agents in a constant stream.

Toby's strategy was predicated on several different elements, all of which were interdependent. All his agents had been assigned. His reserve had long ago been taken up and his mobile force was but a distant memory. All other operations were cancelled and every agent was given a specific role in this operation. The bunker was being run with the minimum number of staff so as to free up more agents. Some of the agents were assigned continued surveillance roles on the North Koreans who had split up into two groups. One group were continually watching the house of one of the scientists and the second group the other. Yet another group of agents remained in place within the power station as maintenance staff and cleaners. This allowed them to contact the two scientists at work and to receive and pass messages to them. Toby had cancelled all leave and days off. As agents were stood down from surveillance roles they were immediately re-deployed on providing protection for the families and loved ones of their fellow agents.

Eventually all the elements were in place. Each person knew their role and also the fact that they were now, every single one of them, in the most acute of dangers.

Clancy's level of consciousness had drifted for some hours. She knew that heavy drinkers were never advised to suddenly stop alcohol without some means of cushioning in the form of drugs, or even to cut down the intake slowly. She realised that she simply did not have enough time to do this and was going to have to go through an abrupt withdrawal.

The night itself was a chain of images, some from her present, many from her past, but all of them acutely disturbing. The abnormal thoughts that were the drink's legacy had magnified the terrors from her past and concurrently had eroded some of the protective defences that she'd built over the years. Moreover, rather than it bringing her rest and recuperation it had only brought to the fore the horrors that her drinking had insulated her from.

She awoke the following day and realised that she was going to have to try to eat something. There was little food in her cabin but she managed to find a couple of eggs of uncertain age. Her trembling hands managed somehow to scramble them in a pan also containing much of the shell. She approached this very slowly and cautiously. Her stomach continued to retch uncontrollably at the very sight of it. After some time in which the eggs had all but cooled she managed to ingest a small amount. Her stomach was still totally attuned to only alcohol and preferable strong spirits. The retching changed to violent vomiting until every last scrap came up along with a lot of fluid that her dehydrated body could have done with retaining. She realised, if such a thing were possible, that she felt even worse for making the attempt. Throughout all this the tremors came to re-exert total control. Her head erupted with more violent headaches that pulsated in synchronisation with her rapidly-firing heart.

All she could do now was to hang on and wonder how long even a partial recovery, if any, would take. She was at least now able to drink cold water without incident and she seized on this like a life-saving serum. She could only wonder, without being aware of the exact threat that faced her ex-colleagues how many of them would still be alive when, and if, she came through.

CHAPTER XIII

Contact

The following day, Dr Crisk was in the turbine hall at Wylfa power station. The room had been partitioned into a glass-walled control room and a further larger room that contained the cold fusion apparatus. This room had been completely stripped out and, in the middle of the empty room, a spherical reaction chamber had been erected made of interlocking panels of precisely-milled, pure Titanium which was six inches thick. These segments had been brought together rather like a chocolate orange albeit a hollow one: one that was immensely strong and was in turn retained and protected by electromagnetic as well as physical forces – thereby allowing the cold fusion process to flicker, to establish itself and, hopefully, to grow. Although the room had obviously been cleared in a hurry, this most definitely did not extend to the reaction vessel, which had been prepared and assembled using every ounce of care at the scientists' disposal. Around this lay arcs of superconducting magnets contained in stainless steel flasks, which were over three metres high. The temperature was as close to absolute zero, nought degrees Kelvin, as modern technology would allow. Such temperatures were required in order to allow for superconductivity in the coils of pure silver wire. This in turn created a focussed magnetic field that was able to support the safe fusion core without utilising any physical contact within the Titanium cauldron.

The vacuum pumps that ran in banks, each adding an extra increment to driving the temperature ever downwards, hissed a little as they carried out their dogged work. The room hummed intrusively with the charge that ran through the superconducting coils and the intense magnetic field so generated.

Most obvious, however, was the steady thrumming noise of the electricity feed that powered the whole apparatus through vast conduits that ran along, and within, the floor causing not just the droning noise but also the walls and floor to vibrate in harmony.

He'd gone in there to check some figures before the preliminary tests were repeated. He stood in front of the wall which was totally taken up with dials, switches and monitoring screens. Banks of indicator lamps and illuminated switches glowed confusingly and intimidatingly as they displayed their status to the few that could interpret such a message.

One of the technicians whom he'd never seen before was also in there. Dr Crisk spoke first, "One can almost detect that history is about to be made in this very room." The other man hadn't really thought about such things; he had a very different agenda and reason for being there that had nothing to do with Thorium reactors or cold fusion. He moved to be a little closer to the scientist so that he would not have to raise his voice over the complex sounds filling the room but, for now, made no attempt to look at him, "Dr Crisk, I am agent Tomkins. I am working for the government, we are here to protect you."

Dr Crisk looked terrified as soon as he heard these words. It brought home to him just how serious a situation he was in. He replied, doing his best to disguise any movement at all from his lips as he hissed through clenched teeth.

"Look, they have our families and they will kill them all unless we do exactly as they say. They follow us both to work. They wait for us when we go home. They are holding my wife hostage and also Mellor's wife and kids. Even talking to you could get them killed – all of them. They appeared a couple of nights ago and now they are camping out in my house watching me, watching us all all continuously. I can't even go to the bathroom on my own."

"We know all about your family. This place is on lockdown since the radiation leak in the old Magnox reactor. As you'll guess, there was no such leak, we just staged it so we could control very carefully who came in and again, as I am sure you realise, that means me and one or two of my colleagues who are here to protect you. You are safe here and the North Koreans won't know that we've had this conversation."

"But my family, what about them?"

"They are also under constant surveillance. Your houses have been bugged and we are monitoring the situation constantly. Those engineers working on the local telephone exchange are all our men. We are aware of the North Koreans' presence and are simply waiting for the right time to intervene; a time when we can catch them off their guard and make sure that you, your family and of course your colleague's family are all kept safe. I need to know what you have been asked to do. Our understanding is that you are to remove blueprints and calculations. How are you to do this?"

"They gave us a solid-state drive, an SSD. We are removing information little by little so that nobody will notice. As soon as we have the entire data set we are to hand over the SSD to the spies, or whatever they are. They say unless we do this then our wives and Mellor's children will be killed. I am terrified, we are all terrified. We are *scientists*, not spies."

"Doctor, I understand what you are saying. That's why we are here. I need to know when the data set will be complete. We plan to act as soon as you hand over the data."

"It's almost done, we will download some files today and also some tomorrow and at that point the SSD will contain a complete set of plans. One mistake and they will kill Mellor and me and and our families."

"We won't let that happen. We are here to protect you all." Tomkins looked grave; there was more, so much more, that the poor man needed to know. He accepted that to burden the poor chap with details of the force that was ranged against them would raise his level of terror up an order of magnitude. The agent decided that to reveal such to the scientist might destabilise him and cause him to behave both erratically and unpredictably with disastrous consequences for all that were involved with the mission and for the people they were trying to protect – quite apart from the precious information that lay at its heart.

"We will be following you, and them, constantly and we are also monitoring both your houses round the clock. I promise as soon as they think they have what they came for we will strike. They can't fly it out, nor can they send any data as the whole Internet is down. We think they will remove the data physically. They will hope to simply drive off the island as soon as they have it, then disappear."

"Can you not arrest them as they drive away with the SSD?"

"No, our strategy will be to intervene as soon as the data is handed over. Our understanding is that this will give us the best chance of retrieving the information and yet keep you all safe." Tomkins did not reveal that their probability studies had shown that once the data had been handed over then the North Koreans best strategy would be to kill them all and quietly make their escape. Moreover, newly-uncovered information held that the North Koreans were the least of their problems. Toby had instructed very carefully that things had to be brought to a head precisely at one single point, and this point would be arrived at as soon as the data drive was produced and handed over.

Someone came in to the cold fusion laboratory.

Tomkins grabbed his clipboard and pretended to write some information from the numerous meters and dials in front of them. As soon as the two men were alone again he continued,

"We are here to protect you and your loved ones. We will all do our level best to do just that. I'll have eyes on you whenever you are in work and other colleagues will take over as soon as you leave and still more when you get home. You will never be out of sight, I promise. We are charged to protect you and your families, to the last man standing if need be."

"Well, I sincerely hope it won't come to that for you or for us."

Tomkins moved away and immediately contacted Toby.

"Channel 2 comms link. It's Tomkins here, Toby, the poor chap is terrified; it's as we thought, his wife is being held hostage, and scientist Mellor's wife and children too.

They are completing the data download over the next 24-48 hours and then they'll be expected to hand it over. The entire data set is being stored on an SSD. This is where everyone's efforts will be concentrated. Things are coming to a head pretty quickly so we don't have much time."

"Understood, Tomkins, many thanks; brief the other agents at the power plant, remember Channel 2 only unless advised otherwise. I'll let you all know by Blackberry Messenger as and when this changes."

Toby terminated the comms link with Tomkins but then immediately contacted other agents to put in place the next phase of his plans. This was the most delicate stage and would be the time when they would be in most danger. From this point on they would all be in the greatest peril with nowhere to hide or to run if things went wrong. Moreover, although Dame Helen had helped with some general support, she had made her position perfectly clear that putting boots on the ground to help them was the last thing she was prepared to do.

Toby communicated with all the agents one by one to make sure that everyone was fully informed and knew the part that he or she was expected to play in the days ahead. He felt more alone now than ever. Inevitably his thoughts turned to Clancy; this would be the part of the mission when he would invariably contact her and ask her views or receive her thoughts and suggestions. How he wished she were here.

Toby wondered how things were going to play out. He'd done his best to run the probability and outcome figures and he'd even enlisted the help of Roger their ablest mathematician and statistician. Roger seemed as apprehensive and sad as Toby; their meeting reminded both men of the person who would normally be present at such time. One who'd smile and laugh as she rubbed her upper lip or chewed her pencil as she thought about the calculations that had been put to her. Then, more often than not, she'd suggest a completely different method of solving the problem and Roger, in particular, would initially not see how this could possibly work; he'd then to stop and assess her suggestions only for it to turn the whole solution on its head. She'd then smile and quietly say that they could do it the original way if they'd prefer only for both men to stare at her open-mouthed. At this point she'd smile more intensely at them, to the point of laughter, as both of them stared now spellbound.

It took every ounce of determination from Toby to keep making progress and gain some degree of order in the chaos that now surrounded them. The hardest part was that mathematical models were at their least helpful when one's adversary was unpredictable and had a habit of resorting to extreme violence almost as a default position. Notwithstanding this was the fact that Toby recognised that the only advantage they possessed, because of Tim's forward thinking, was that of surprise. Toby was going to make sure that they used such a gift to its utmost and for sure they were not going down without a fight. His mind wandered back to missions that he'd experienced alongside Clancy where they faced similar appalling odds and yet had still managed to come through. Toby planned to stay in contact with all the agents and make sure that they were all as well-briefed as possible. Once again, he spent most of the night passing information and instructions to his agents.

Only when this had been done did he skype Alexis. He glanced briefly at the clock and saw that it was well into the early hours of the new day.

"Hi, my love, I was just thinking about you and I thought I'd phone you before I went to bed."

Alexis blinked sleepy eyes until they registered the time.

"Okay, Toby, that's wonderful, and it's also two in the morning."

Alexis had an important meeting later the same day and she knew that Toby knew this too.

"You know I always love to hear from you even when I've been in bed for two whole hours."

"Sorry, my love, something came up and I realised that I had to tell you."

"Oh oh, okay, now I am fully awake and you have my *undivided* attention. So, what's on your mind?"

Alexis knew Toby so well that he should have been aware that she would see the hidden agenda behind his words and the delicate pauses. Silence opened as he furiously thought what he could tell her.

"Go on, you might as well tell me. I can tell there's something going on, so you might as well get it off your chest. You're not calling everything off, are you?"

Toby laughed, "No, honey, that's the last thing on my mind."

"Good start, so you'd better just keep talking, then."

"Oh, I just needed to hear your voice."

"Go on, I am listening. And?"

"It's just that a mission has gone badly awry. I need you to do something for me."

More often than not, she'd agree without question, under ordinary circumstances. However, she knew by a simple glance at his gaunt image on screen that these were far from ordinary circumstances.

"Okay then, now we are getting somewhere. What do we mean exactly, badly awry?

So, are you in danger?"

"Yes, we are all in danger. It's such an important thing and yet it seemed so simple at first; then we came to realise just what, and whom, we are up against. These people literally will take no prisoners; they will kill us all on a whim. I know how they work; I've seen it so many times from the other side. We can't pull out; many will die if we do, and the country will lose vital secrets. We may not be able to stop it anyway, but we have to do our best."

His tone of voice frightened her. She wondered if she could go to him so that they would be together come what may.

"Whoa, Toby, slow down. Just tell me slowly. What can be so important, so dangerous and why can't you pull out if things have gone that badly? Surely you can *always* pull out?"

She knew just by looking at him that this was something else, something of such overarching importance that people would kill for it and also be expected to die for it.

"So, Toby, why is that? Why not just pull out and let someone else handle it?"

"We promised we would see it through."

"Sometimes promises have to be broken when things change. No-one can expect you to lay your life down, surely this is why we have a government and things called *security* forces; can we not get a few of them out of bed?"

"We can't; we said we would do it. We are working for the Government, for the Nation, but we cannot be seen to be doing so. We are doing their dirty work for them. Besides, even backing out would make no difference; our foes know everything, where we are, who we are and where our loved ones are. It's gone too far for us to pull out. We are inextricably linked and it's all our fault."

"How can they know all that? Why do you say it's your fault, how can that be? And why am I not surprised that you've been dropped in it?"

"We let them in. They don't know that we know just yet but this won't last long. We are expected to commit the whole force, if need be, and each of us is expendable. Look, I haven't got much time, I need to convey more instructions to the agents and I have to do it now so they can start planning immediately, I just need you to know that I love you and I need you to do something for me, please." There it was again, that beseeching tone. Her mind raced; things must be really bad for him to be at such a low ebb. Moreover, he looked exhausted.

More questions brimmed with urgency; she started to run through them.

He stopped her. He knew she needed more, much more, and surely deserved as much, and yet he'd run out of time; there was still so much to do and it had to be done now. He could only hope that she could both forgive him and trust him in equal measure.

"Sorry, my darling, but there are two things I need you to do urgently. I'm sorry there isn't enough time for me to go into it." Moreover, he couldn't reveal the main reason for them all to be in such danger. His only hope was to keep her in the dark for her own safety and to get her as far away as the situation allowed and hope that it would be far enough.

"Toby, you are really frightening me. What do you need me to do? If only Penny was here."

"I know, my love, I feel the same way, but she's too ill."

"Alexis, do you remember what I told you to do if I didn't come back from a mission and how to access the safe? Do you remember the access code and how I showed you what to do?"

"No, Toby, I don't want to remember any of those things. I want *you* to tell me them ever so slowly, and every single day for many years to come, until we are both in our dotage. At that time we'll pass on those secrets to our five kids."

"Five kids, Alexis, bloody hell, you didn't tell me you wanted five kids!"

"At least, my love, so you see you aren't going to have the time to go out on these dangerous missions when you'll have all of us to look after."

He laughed but his moment of light-heartedness was cut short by the matters that weighed upon him and indeed all of them.

"Look, Alexis, I need you to get in that safe and grab the documents and the information in there. Alexis, you are not secure either. The *Ma Puissance* is en-route from Italy making all speed to Cavtat and I want you to get the next flight out to

Dubrovnik as soon as your meeting is over. I have detailed Monty to help; he is the only one I can spare and I need to activate him tonight or he won't be in place. I need you to help him, my love, to save as many as we can. Are you able to do this for me?"

He knew that this was a good way to secure Alexis' assistance, by informing her that she was needed to help out and to save others. He waited what seemed like an age before the reluctant nod appeared. He did his best to control his breathing so that she would not notice the sigh that he would otherwise have given off out of sheer relief. "Nobody is safe, they'll have every single one in their sights as soon as they are able and they could be starting tonight. I need to get you out and protect many others. You can help Monty and all the others.

I have to get on with those calls now as I have to brief so many. Can I count on you?"

"Toby, it's not right and it's not fair." She just had to return to the facts that troubled her the most. "I don't see why you should be in this degree of danger?"

"Nobody said it was fair, it's just how it is. It's just the way things have played out and I can't change it."

"But how did they know so much about you, about all of you?" The pause brought the answer to her question. "Oh, no! Don't tell me! I should have guessed, this is why you've got yourselves in such a pickle. I knew there was something you weren't telling me! I could laugh and cry at the same time. I am *so* going to go on about this, all of it, for a long, long time to come, you just wait until I see you. In that case, can I not stay with you and help to plan your countermeasures? I can help."

"Look, my love, you are right; we brought this on ourselves. I need to know you are safe and also that the information that you take with you is safe."

"Please, Alexis, can you do this for me?" Ultimately it was his expression that allowed her to accept both his words and the strategy he was trying to put in place. She knew that not co-operating would impose more worry on his overwrought mind and this was why he looked as dreadful as he did. Furthermore, she just had to take his suggestion that she was needed to save the others at face value. Her eyes widened; she stared and then nodded. Once again he suppressed a sigh of sheer relief.

"Very well, but I'll be *expecting* you to join me as soon as you can."

"I will, my love, it's a promise."

She knew there was no conviction in his words; it was a promise he could not keep, unlike the one that was threatening his very life that he *was* expected to keep. Moreover, she suspected that the information she was to take with her was simply a ruse to get her out of harm's way – if such a thing were still possible. How could they, all of them, have been so stupid? Only Miss Clancy had seen, or so it seemed, what was in store for them and perhaps it was this.

"Oh, and inside the safe you'll find a communicator, just the standard type we all use. Charge it then pop it in your ear, the way you've seen me do. Very important, please set it to channel 2 and please keep it active at all times, or at least until you get to the Puissance. Get to Cavtat as soon as you can."

"Sounds like a repeat of when the Russians were after us...."

"Yes, as they say, history doesn't repeat itself but sometime it rhymes."

"Well, it's rhyming now and to me it doesn't sound very nice. I can't believe you let this befall you just when you were making progress. You keep yourself safe and meet me as soon as you can. I'll have the G&Ts stacked on the sun deck waiting for you so *don't* let me down."

"I won't. I'm sorry my love, I have to go."

He terminated the link.

Alexis sat there for a minute or two and then realised it was still the early hours of the morning. She knew that she'd pay for her wakefulness now the following day. However, her meeting seemed much less important, given the lens through which she now viewed things. She would open the safe in the way that he'd shown her, and extract the contents, as soon as she could and then make her escape as he'd requested. She'd also seen how they fitted and used the new communicators, although she'd never been asked to change the channel before. Only with some further thought did she guess why. It was true that Toby was playing a very dangerous game. One that could either see them all come through or cause a heavy casualty rate if he failed, or in fact made the slightest miscalculation.

She was tortured so much, as she tried to gain some more sleep, about the importance of selecting the right channel, that she got up and wrote a list of the things she had to extract from the safe and how to reset the communicator for the new channel. Only then did she even attempt to get some sleep and succeeded for about half an hour before her early alarm went off. Toby had also told her that vital information would be passed to her and that she should keep the communicator charged, active and on her at all times.

CHAPTER XIV

Trigger Happy

Other early risers were the Wainwrights. Tim rose early as he was due to join the mission in Wales. His mum had cooked breakfast that nobody seemed to want. Mariah looked on somewhat redundantly as the older woman fussed round her menfolk doing her best to encourage Tim, in particular, to eat something. Arthur did his best to try to busy himself with the newspaper but made very little progress as his thoughts were still with the danger that Tim, and indeed all of them, now seemed to be in.

Tim received a secure message on his Blackberry. He could see that messages were coming in thick and fast as more of the agents were made aware of the danger they faced. Above all he knew that he'd better keep the device charged and with him at all times. Although these devices were old by modern standards, the Blackberry servers and messaging were thought to be unbreakable and would allow for secure and restricted messages while Toby began to hone his response to the threats now facing them. Tim acknowledged the message and briefed his parents as to what they could expect and what would happen after he had gone. They listened with incredulity but nevertheless agreed to co-operate in whatever way they could.

Tim journeyed to Anglesey. As he drove in the fresh and misty morning he realised that Toby had done his utmost, not only to respond to any likelihood, but also to protect as many loved ones as his stretched resources allowed. Tim was due to be briefed by Brady. He met up with him in a small restaurant just on the outskirts of Amlwch which had been purportedly closed for refurbishment but in fact had been taken over by Horizon so that they could use it as a forward operations base.

Janet was also present when Tim entered. She kissed him passionately so much so that even Brady, not one to be easily shocked, blushed, his pale complexion flaring against his red hair.

"Nice to see you too, Janet."

"Gee, lover, been missing you."

"Okay, if I could have your attention," Brady's voice barked out a little more emphatically than usual so as to refocus everyone's minds from other distractions.

Stephens stood in front of the whiteboard that had been erected in the restaurant.

His laptop and projector displayed images. The screen displayed up to the minute surveillance footage of the scientists, scenes from within the power station and, crucially, covert surveillance that had been set up within the scientists' homes. Moreover, everyone's movement was tracked, especially that of the North Koreans who were now never without a pair of Horizon eyes on them.

By bringing together all this information, and also the likely sequence of events, agents were, as far as possible, prepared and trained for the intervention that Horizon planned to take.

Toby joined them a little later the same day so as to add the last minute fine-tuning that the operation demanded.

"Well, things are much clearer now. Our visitors from Pyongyang have split into two groups and, we believe, have taken Crisk's wife hostage, they have no children, and Mellor's family has also been taken hostage. He has two children. We checked with the local school and they've been told that the family are holidaying in Australia. The wife and kids are kept hostage; nobody has been allowed to leave the house apart from our two boffins. Four North Koreans are in each house and the other four have been placed on surveillance duties making sure that they get to work each day and home each night.

The foreign agents have not been able to infiltrate Wylfa; security is too tight.

Our team of *cleaners* are on-site round the clock. One of those is agent Tomkins who has made regular contact with both Crisk and Mellor. Sensitive data about the plans and the specifications and the design of the reactor vessels is being removed slowly and the whole thing is then being recombined on to an SSD which, we assume, the North Koreans will try to smuggle off the island. Owing to the efforts of Dame Helen, this has been made extremely difficult and the only way, since the Internet and mobile comms have been brought down, is by trafficking it physically off the island.

Dame Helen really came through for us. Apparently there has been a fire at the conduits that convey telephone lines, cable and the Internet, of course. This means that even mobile signals have gone down together with all land based comms. Word is that the 'fire' was so bad that it will take a week or so. In another terrible blow, *for our adversaries*, RAF Valley are testing a new type of helicopter so that the MOD have had to close airspace above the whole island. This has raised one or two problems for our visitors as we believe the only way out is either exfiltration by sea, which they will not have the resources to mount, or physically carrying data off the island.

Crisk and Mellor are taking it in turns to download information a little at a time. This is to keep any such activity below the radar and not trigger any suspicions from the on-site security force. Tomkins has briefed them in any event but not revealed such to the two scientists who are both very shaky and feel that, the more people who know, the more in danger their loved ones will be.

Our guess is that, once they have the data, our North Korean friends will disappear quickly. Although we have blocked off one or two rat runs, we cannot assume that they don't have some contingency plans. Also, do not forget that they discovered somehow that our cold-fusion plant was here on this quiet island, tucked away, and very, very few knew that. What else do they know, and what resources can they count on? For this reason we cannot let that data out of our sight nor them. Four agents are watching each house round the clock. Our cameras are inside and outside the buildings and the control room is monitoring such footage continuously. We have two teams following the North Koreans as they follow the scientists to work and back again in the evening. We will then have further fresh strike teams to intervene in both houses simultaneously as soon as the SSD is finalised and handed over to the foreign agents. Timing will be crucial and a drift in this will endanger innocent lives.

Our plan, therefore, begins tomorrow at daybreak, as soon as the boffins have left for work. I have allocated two teams who will follow each of the scientists to work. We will continue with the personnel rotation just in case someone is recognised. The North Koreans escort them and then usually wait for them, just beyond the gatehouse, as they leave for the day. They then escort them home. Our teams will simply shadow them. Tomkins can pass last minute instructions on to Crisk and Mellor at work. They are going to be very nervous as their wives and Mellor's kids are held hostage for the entire time they are at work. The poor devils must have been through hell in the past few days.

We are told that tomorrow Crisk will bring home the complete SSD. Our studies indicate at this time the visitors will verify the data and then make their escape. It will be easier from their point of view at this point if they simply kill everyone as, for them, this indicates the best chance of success and subsequent escape. Of course, they do not know that we know and will intervene as soon as they get home.

We've prepared two attack teams. Janet you are to lead Team one; remember you will go in to Crisk's house and it will be your job to secure the SSD or destroy it. Of course it goes without saying that the safety of Dr and Mrs Crisk should be given the greatest priority. Can you do this for me Janet?

Remember, keep your communications link open at all times, channel one.

Team two, Tim I'd like you to lead this attack force at Mellor's house. It is essential that you attack at the same time. We cannot be certain that the North Koreans have not devised a mission failure signal of some description, which is why the second house must be secured at the same time as the first. As you know, there will be two kids in the house and of course Mrs Mellor, all being threatened and held hostage. Once again, the safety of all of them is of paramount importance."

"Don't worry Toby, I will come through for you, I promise."

"I know that, Tim, I have every confidence in you, and in you, Janet. It's vital that timing is to the second to maximise surprise and hopefully minimise casualty rates. Regard the visitors as expendable if we have to but, of course, get the boffins and their families well out of the way and those two kids, in particular, must be removed as a priority in case the whole mission gets away from us."

Janet was clearly not very happy. She paced up and down like a caged lion.

"Why wait until tomorrow? I can get down there now and kick some ass. A few lousy North Koreans will be no match for my Glock," which she then proceeded to brandish menacingly in front of them all. They all hastily looked to see if the safety was off. Rumour had it that she never used the safety lock so that she would be in a position to shoot someone at the first offing. "I can get in there tonight and finish this thing."

"No, Janet, the scenarios that we have run show that we have a much higher chance of securing the data, and of protecting the hostages and our scientists, if we strike as soon as the North Koreans believe they have succeeded. This is going to be their weak spot, the point of success, and by this time, they will have fully committed themselves and also any other resources, if any, they have to call upon. We need to know that we can ensnare everyone. It's the only way to maximise our chances and conclude the operation neatly. It's also important that you don't strike until we are all ready. Mellor's house has to be secured at the same time and that, Tim, is where you and Brady come in. He has children and the situation there could easily get out of hand. There will be no information there but we don't know if the foreign agents will use them as extra leverage and threaten to kill the kids unless scientist one co-operates.

I am sorry I am labouring my point," he tried, but inevitably failed, not to look at Janet in that moment; everyone knew why, but her, "but I need to make sure that everyone is clear on this?" He now looked round the room and made sure that his gaze did not alight on Janet for too long.

Janet remained standing throughout; she paced the room, making them all feel even more nervous. Her walking seemed to make her more anxious, not less. She continually rubbed the pink band of the Fitbit device round her left wrist as she did so.

Eventually Toby said in his most soothing tones that he struggled with, "Janet, it's vital that we are all singing from the same hymn sheet here. You understand why the timing is crucial if we are to keep the casualty count to a minimum. Please remember too that you will be recovering the SSD. Your role is therefore crucial to the whole mission. I need to know that I can count on you, Janet? Our information is that Crisk has been asked to take it home with him. It's vital, Janet, that you don't let this get away from you as the whole mission revolves around its safe retrieval or at least its destruction."

She glared at Toby, still far from happy.

"Yeh, yeh, Toby, I know what I gotta do. Just sayin' I could get round there, now." Toby looked at her carefully as she continued, "Oh, I'll have them singing tomorrow, don't you worry, Toby." She rammed her Glock back into its holster, rubbed her left wrist agitatedly again, and she went out of the room.

Tim hung back. Toby lowered his voice conspiratorially, "Tim, we have one chance. Yours is going to be the most difficult role. You realise, I'm sure, that all our lives now depend on you. Nobody, none of them must get an inkling. Are you sure you want this? You don't want me to do it?"

"No, Toby, thank you, but it has to be me. Oh, don't worry, Toby it's the least I can do. I will do my bit, I promise and I won't let you down. I will also do my best to make sure the data does not go astray or at least that it is destroyed."

"In that case you'll need this."

Toby handed over a gleaming valise made from smooth, elemental aluminium.

Tim caressed its fine lines with the flat of his hand as if he were stroking the flank of a thoroughbred racehorse. He looked at the chromed and slightly raised panels at either side of the case.

"I haven't seen one of these before."

"This, Tim, is the mark 2; it's a new and improved version for highly sensitive or very precious contents. I suspect you'll need something like it. Toby pointed to a tiny red-plastic wedge set in the frame of the case. Please don't remove this until you are ready. I'll explain how it works."

A minute or two later, Tim nodded his head out of recognition that he not only knew how the case worked but also that he understood Toby's motives in giving it to him.

"You realise that as soon as you close the case, you will be in very great danger. You and everyone in that room."

"I understand and I am prepared to do whatever is required."

"Of course, I hope it won't come down to that...." Toby said gravely.

"Toby, it's a good plan and I will come through for you. Having brought this upon us it's fitting that I am the one to end it.

Toby, do you think...do you think if Miss Clancy were here she'd think I'd let you all down?"

"No, Tim, most definitely not. Clancy would say what we all say; that we are proud to be working alongside you. She knew, right from the start, when she begged me to make you an offer to join us; and she wasn't wrong. I'm giving you that case and this role because I know that I can count on you. Please don't think that anyone blames you, because that could not be further from the truth and if Clancy were here, then she'd be the first to say it."

"If I don't come through, Toby, will you tell her; can you tell her how I stepped up?"

"Tim, I hope that one day, one day very soon, you'll be able to tell her yourself. In truth, if you don't come through then it's unlikely many of the agents will."

"But, Toby, *if* you can and I can't, will you do that for me?" The point was obviously so important to his younger colleague; Toby finally grasped just how important it was.

"Tim, yes, yes of course."

"We'll plot for 8 am but, in truth, we can't start until the boffins are underway." Tim was about to leave the room and find Janet. Toby tapped the case just before he turned to go. "Better let me keep that, perhaps collect it from me later?" Toby smiled and Tim could only acknowledge, with a little nod and a weak smile, that Toby had probably just saved his life. "Oh, yes, yes, of course I'll collect it later. Thanks, Toby, and thanks for everything..." the pause denoted words that Tim could not voice; redundant words, in any case, that Toby understood without the medium of speech, marking the sentiments with a nod of his own. Tim left while Toby turned his attention to the remainder of his agents who would accompany Janet in the first team and Tim in the second. He went through final details with them all but his last words just before their meeting broke up were with Brady. "I'm sure I don't have to tell you that things could get very ugly and your team, you and Tim will be in most danger. Whichever way I run it, it comes down to that point. I wish there was a better way."

"Don't you worry, Toby, I agree that, of all the scenarios that could have played out, this gives us the best chance of success and with minimal casualties. We'll be fine, Toby, and I agree with you, Tim is the best person for the job."

Once again, words failed, there was now only time for deeds that would either carry the day or mean the deaths of so many experienced, loyal and trusted agents. Toby held out his hand and it was enfolded by Brady's much larger palm. The meeting was over, plans were laid and now all they could do was wait for the following day.

CHAPTER XV

Visitors

It was 1 pm and Margaret had been eating for no more than five minutes in the kitchen. She was glued to the CCTV screen that monitored the front gate. She knew that the person she was expecting would not be late, even though she'd never met him before. Bang on time the buzzer was activated.

"Mrs Wainwright? My name is Griff, you should be expecting me?"

"Yes indeed, Griff, as soon as you give me the password I've been told to ask you for."

Griff smiled, "Yes, of course. Password is 'guest appearance'."

She pressed the button and massive gates began to swing with their quiet and unfussed motion.

"We have left our cars out on the drive; if you go to the rear of the house you will find the garage doors are open. You can put your car in there, Griff."

"Righto, Mrs W."

Margaret asked him if he fancied anything to eat, which he declined, but he did accept a cup of tea. Mariah, for once, was allowed to get on with the job that she was paid to do and within a couple of minutes she placed a steaming mug of tea in front of the Horizon agent.

Toby had thought hard and long about the mission and also recognised the constant danger they would all face. Mercifully, Dame Helen's help, although firmly kept in the background at all times, was, nevertheless, crucial. The masterstroke, however, as adjudged by Toby was to make sure using their open communication channel one that all the agents knew exactly where everyone was at all times. This might well carry the day. As with all plans, however, things could never be predicted with perfect accuracy, and at times casualty rates could climb alarmingly.

Alexis had reluctantly responded to Toby's plea that she should open and then empty the safe, taking the items therein in a secure and armed attaché case, which she placed on the passenger seat while she drove to her meeting. As soon as her meeting was finished she drove directly towards Manchester airport. Toby had asked her to take the back road rather than the motorway. Almost at once she was aware of a dark car following her. Toby had warned her of such a likelihood. This is why he wanted her out of the way; her very reason for approaching the airport. She did her best to keep calm, yet with each turn and each bend she became more focussed on the constant image in her mirror and less on the road in front of her. She did her best to concentrate, to suppress the feeling of panic rising within and to negotiate the winding roads carefully; eventually the airport was within sight. As she approached the terminal, a long straight road lay in front of her followed by a final tight bend after which she would be able to drive into the terminal car park.

Just as she drove along this straight section, the following car accelerated and deliberately rammed into her. The sound of the collision went off like an explosion within the confines of her car. She gripped the steering wheel just as the seatbelt pretensioners held her back in her seat. The unexpected event caused her to sway violently across the road so much so that she nearly collided head on with a car coming the other way. The approaching car sounded his horn both loud and long and, for good measure, gave her an obscene gesture as they passed. She panicked; she could see them men in the car behind her making ready for another run.

Even worse, however, she could see that the pursuing car had started to drive across the road. This allowed the front seat passenger to lean out of the window, and Alexis could see that he carried an assault rifle. She was now gripped, both by fear and by the scene that was unfolding in her rear view mirror that she struggled to take her eyes off. A few shots were loosed off by her pursuer as he used the door as a support; the rifle giving off a sharp clackety-clack sound like a firework. The bullets thudded into the road behind her but were very close. A strand of logic in the unbridled panic held that they were attempting to shoot out her tyres.

Suddenly, her communicator burst into life.

"Hi, Alexis. I'm here to help you. I can see you. I need you to accelerate as quickly and as soon as you are able. I also want you to drive in a zig-zag fashion as far as the oncoming traffic will allow. You must try to deny them those shots. They are trying to take out your tyres but one of those bullets could easily…."

The pause said it all, Alexis realised without its being confirmed to her that any of those many bullets issuing forth from the gun could bounce up and hit her car, or indeed her. Her worse fear was that the petrol tank might be hit by a glancing bullet, and she couldn't suppress the grisly thought of whether she'd have enough time to stop and clear the car before the whole thing went up. Notwithstanding this, the presence of another, one sent by Toby, looking out for her, and there to protect her gave Alexis a significant boost to her confidence and allowed her to calm, just a little, her racing heart.

"Toby warned me I might be followed. They have been behind me for much of the way here. I didn't realise they would ram me and start shooting. Are they trying to get me to stop?"

"Yes, that's exactly what they want and this is why I need you to go *faster*, at least for the moment, and also zig-zag if you can; it will frustrate them a great deal. I am watching you and them. They won't be following you for much longer. Toby anticipated that so many would be followed in this way. It's how they work. Please listen carefully. I am here to help you, that's why Toby sent me. All I need you to do, Alexis, is to follow my instructions and I will do the rest. Begin now, Alexis, accelerate as fast as you can and then slow to a crawl through that last bend and I will do the rest."

She pressed the accelerator and the Evoque dropped down a couple of gears as the revs rose together with the power output and, most vitally, her speed. She gulped, she could hardly breathe. Panic continued to consume her as she felt her grip on the steering wheel loosen with the trembling and the sweat that seemed to issue unfailingly from her palms and much of the rest of her body.

"Alexis, there isn't much time. You see the bend ahead of you. I want you to turn as sharply into the right-hander as you are able. Most importantly, I want you to brake at this point for all you're worth, slow to a crawl. You will be out of their field of fire as you turn into the bend. They won't be able to overtake you, although they may collide again with you so be prepared for that. I am ready and waiting for them."

Alexis looked at the passenger seat; it had all the information that Toby had asked her to retrieve from the safe inside a sealed case. She braked as instructed and the all-round discs slowed the red Evoque, giving off brake-pad dust and some smoke as they did so, just as she was about to enter the last bend. The black Mondeo was following so closely at this point that it was all the driver could do to avoid crashing into the rear end of the Evoque. The anti-lock braking system pulsated quickly and intrusively under the driver's right foot as it sought to gain the maximum braking in such a short distance.

Meanwhile, the super yacht, Ma Puissance, was running with all speed to make Cavtat harbour to pick up not only her but other wives, fiancées and partners too. The engineer was muttering below decks that over-running the engines in this way was not good for them especially so soon following their service. Captain Richards was insistent, however, and this was an unusual thing in itself, therefore the engineer did his best to keep his mutterings to himself and did all he could to keep an eye on them as they churned intrusively with more noise than had previously been experienced either by him or by any of the crew. At the same time, Bill Richards had the crew on deck. Each of them had been issued with a revolver and the sun deck had been converted into a firing range. As soon as he was happy that they could all hit a static target, then he arranged for the launch to run alongside the super yacht towing a further target, in scenes reminiscent of shooting practice as carried out by the Royal Navy in Nelson's time, when gun crews were asked to hit empty barrels. None of the crew wanted to steer the launch saying it was too dangerous, so the captain made sure they used a long length of line to tow the target and that they each took turns to pilot the launch. Accuracy of shooting improved beautifully as a result.

Back in Manchester, Alexis was transfixed by the precipitous and violent images contained in her rear-view mirror. Paradoxically, her sudden and unforeseen movements unsettled the driver of the black Mondeo who now found himself braking in unison with Alexis so as to avoid a collision, as his colleague was leaning from the passenger window attempting to shoot out her tyres. Eventually, after what seemed like an age, the Mondeo's speed was brought down allowing for the avoidance of a collision and, also, a safer distance opened up between it and the Evoque. Just as the pursuing driver eased off on the brake, the front tyre burst. The car veered wildly but remained on the road as the driver struggled to regain control. It was all his passenger could do to hang on and avoid both losing grip of his weapon and being jettisoned from the car via the fully open window. Just when both pursuers thought that things could get no worse, the rear tyre on the same side burst explosively. The gift from this catastrophic occurrence, even at a reducing speed, was that the car became dangerously unstable and no amount of wrestling with the steering wheel from the driver could keep them from veering off the road completely. The car only stopped after crossing the grass verge and demolishing a couple of sections of the perimeter fence of the airport. Neither of the occupants of the pursuing vehicle were wearing seatbelts. They managed to vacate the stricken Mondeo but they were badly shaken, especially the passenger who, in the violent excursions of movement had dropped his assault rifle.

The communicator burst into life once again. "Alexis, that's sorted them; you are safe now. Please do *not* go to Manchester, take the exit road instead and on to the motorway. Please head for Liverpool, John Lennon. Repeat, divert immediately from Manchester. Monty is waiting for you and for many others. Please take the confidential files that Toby mentioned, with you. The plane will take off as soon as everyone is there."

"Understood, I have the files here with me." Alexis looked again at the passenger seat with the beautiful, smooth aluminium case upon it as she spoke. "I am diverting as requested. I'll go and help Monty. Thank you for getting rid of my pursuers; I hope they got their just desserts." She touched the communicator as she spoke, almost hoping this would add emphasis to her words. "Don't worry about us, just keep yourselves safe and…" she hesitated, but the Horizon agent had already anticipated what she was about to say, "and keep Toby safe."

"Understood, Alexis, good luck."

As soon as she saw Alexis's red Evoque take up the new directions, the young woman with the high velocity rifle quickly disassembled her weapon and placed it in a holdall. She ran down a side street to her waiting car. As she did so, she pressed a button on her comms link. "Channel 2. Mission carried out. One totally-disabled Mondeo on the approach to Manchester airport and two badly-shaken bad guys. Alexis is on her way to Liverpool."

Toby responded immediately, as if he had been waiting for her message. "Well done, Tracy, proceed to meet up with Griff as arranged. Let me know when you are in position."

A short time later, Tracy appeared in her car in the CCTV monitoring the Wainwright front entrance gates. She introduced herself and offered the password that Margaret had asked her for. Once again, the substantial gates began to move on their no less substantial bearings with their noiseless majesty. She, too, drove her car into the garage and the doors were closed.

Margaret sat both agents down in the morning room and Mariah brought another cup of tea. "Toby phoned me and told me that this is purely a precaution."

"Yes indeed, Mrs Wainwright," Tracy nodded between taking sips of her hot tea.

"Please call me Margaret?"

"We know how these people work. They don't come at you directly, they seek to weaken you catastrophically and then they strike. We have seen this so many times over the years, though it's unusual that we are on the receiving end." Griff looked at Tracy who nodded her elfin head with its short black hair in complete agreement, her expression still a little flushed with her recent labours.

"Yes, I couldn't believe it when Tim told me, and these people are supposed to be our friends? What do they do to their enemies?"

"That's it, Margaret, when anyone gets in their way they become an enemy. That is why all of us are in danger. Of course, they may not come here at all. In fact there may be others that will receive visits. We have simply protected as many as we could, either by flying them out or by adding some cover."

"For which we thank you most sincerely," came from Arthur as he listened attentively.

"In any event, if they do make a strike they will do so within 24 hours."

Later that same afternoon the buzzer on the front gate was activated again and Margaret saw a young couple in black suits standing there.

"Oh, is this the Wainwright residence? We've been sent by Toby Richmond, ma'am. I can explain more in a minute but you are in grave danger."

"Very well, in that case you'd better come inside."

Their black car parked in front of the house and Mariah showed them into the living room. Arthur sat reading the paper and Margaret resumed sipping her cup of tea.

"I'm Brandon and this is my colleague, Teresa. Is there anyone else at home, ma'am?"

"No, just me, Arthur and Mariah, of course."

"Are you sure, no one else?" Queried Teresa, as she looked around agitatedly.

"Yes, of course, but why?

"Oh nothing, Mrs Wainwright, we just have to make sure that you are all accounted for…so that we can protect you." came almost as an afterthought.

Mariah appeared with more tea and set it down on the small table.

"But why do we need protection?" came from Margaret.

"Well, ma'am, it has to be said that there are some nasty people out there who will hurt you all unless you do exactly as they say. Brandon lunged forwards at this point and grabbed both Mariah's arms just as she turned to go. He pulled them behind her so savagely that she screamed in pain.

"Restrain her, Teresa."

Margaret jumped, and Arthur too, as they saw their stunned maid in distress.

Teresa pulled a large cable tie over Mariah's wrists and pulled it tight until the poor woman yelped in pain again.

"Do not hurt poor Mariah; just who are you and what do you want from us?"

"You will not be harmed as long as you do everything we ask. Our purpose here is simply to make sure that your son, Tim, does everything that we require of him." Teresa had a steely dispassionate look about her. Inflicting such pain on Mariah had not even caused her to blink, as she stared at Margaret now with some menace.

"Are you all right, Mariah?" Margaret asked of her.

Mariah nodded a little awkwardly, but grimaced as she tried to adjust the plastic ties that were cutting into her wrists.

"It's going to be a day or two, so we may as well all make ourselves comfortable," suggested Brandon.

Brandon and Teresa pulled a couple of single chairs out and sat on them facing the older couple. Both of them produced hand guns and placed them on their laps with an undisguised menace. The look on Brandon's face, in particular, more than hinted at his enjoyment over the discomfiture of their three hostages

"You won't be needing *those*," came from Arthur, his eyes flaring with alarm.

"I do hope not, Arthur, do you mind if I call you Arthur?" he said a little disrespectfully.

"Well, Arthur, that depends on you and, of course, on your son doing exactly what we tell him to do."

"Who are you?" Interruped Margaret .

"We represent people who want what you've got."

"Who, us? And what do you mean, something that we have? Surely you mean something that the Government has or the nation has?"

"Yes, I suppose that's fair. Only it won't be for much longer. We are gonna take it by whatever means necessary."

"Well, before you do that, if you don't mind, I need to visit the bathroom," volunteered Arthur a little ostentatiously as he then stood up a little awkwardly. "My bladder is not what it used to be, especially when I'm stressed."

Brandon stood, too, and placed the revolver in his rear waist band.

"You don't mean you are going to come with me?"

"Yes, I sure am, old timer. We can't have you doing something stupid and endangering everyone, including or especially your son. He might then do something stupid and get lots of people shot and you two will be the first of many to die." He nodded unconcernedly.

"No, I suppose not, off we go then. Let's go and water the horse."

Arthur led the way out of the room and Brandon followed closely behind. A few minutes later, Arthur returned and walked to stand by Margaret. He also asked Mariah if she was all right.

"Where's Brandon?" asked Teresa, a hint of alarm just beginning to form as she sensed that her colleague had been detained by something or someone.

"Oh, he's right behind," offered Arthur's soothing tones.

Sensing that something was wrong she stood up and reached for her gun. As she was about to do so a female voice appeared from behind her.

"No, no, touch that gun and I'm afraid it will be the last thing you do, just let it fall to the floor, then sit down again, please."

Teresa looked around and saw Tracy standing there. She saw the Glock pointed in her direction aimed straight at her head. "Please kick your gun forwards and then place your arms behind the chair." Tracy grabbed both her arms and applied restraints with a satisfying click.

At this point Brandon came in with Griff just behind.

"Griff nodded to Teresa. Please don't get up on my account."

"You might want to sit down, too, Brandon," suggested Tracy. Teresa could see that he'd been relieved of his handgun and it was now tucked in the front of Griff's trousers.

Griff cuffed Brandon, his arms being pulled behind him with similar treatment to that which they had unleashed on Mariah. Tracy pulled out a knife and used it to cut through the cable ties around the maid's wrists. Mariah gasped as the band was released. She then rubbed her wrists until the soreness began to fade.

"I am so sorry about that, Mariah, my love. If you want to leave early then that's fine by me or, if you would like to stay, then I'll make you a nice cup of tea. Please sit down by my side." Margaret said, patting the cushion.

Mariah informed her boss that she would like to stay and saw no reason to leave with things in such turmoil. Thinking that she'd feel better keeping to her routines, she went into the kitchen to make more tea.

Griff was a large, towering man. He seemed even larger as he stood in the middle of the room just before Brandon.

"Now then, we all know how this works. Is there a regular check-in that you have to make or a mission compromised signal?"

"Go, fuck yourself."

"Brandon, that is very ungentlemanly talk, especially with ladies present."

"I'm not going to tell you limey bastard rookies zip. Go and fuck yourself."

"Forgive me, Margaret, is the chair expensive?" He asked as he screwed the silencer into the end of the Glock.

"No, not at all."

While still looking at Margaret, Griff fired his extended revolver seemingly without looking at Brandon. The shell thudded explosively into the chair but between his legs and millimetres from his genitals.

"That always works better on the men," he said with satisfaction.

"Now then, Brandon, the next one will be a bit higher and I suppose it's safe to say that if you value your continence, not to mention anything else that the organ in question might be used for, then you'd better start talking in the next few seconds. Besides, my second shot is never quite as good as the first; I dare say the bullet could go anywhere." With this he waved his gun around as if trying to focus an unsteady aim.

"Oh, you fucker, you nearly shot me."

"That will be my *next* shot, Brandon, and I am afraid there isn't much time. You know that the stakes are high and that we will do anything, *anything* to protect Tim and our fellow agents. Sadly, that includes shooting the two of you if you don't give us reasons not to in the next few minutes. Now, what's it to be?"

Tracy now stood in front of Teresa and levelled her weapon.

"Can I try that, Griff? You said it was my turn to shoot the bad guy. Now where does the bullet come out?"

Teresa screamed as Tracy deliberately weaved the gun in an uncontrolled way as if the shot could have gone anywhere.

"No, there's no regular check in, only if we failed to make contact."

"Thank you for that Teresa. Now, Tracy, if you'd empty our guest's pockets and I'll do the same with Brandon."

"Whadya tell these limeys for?"

"What! And get shot. I don't think so, besides it's too late for them to do much now anyways."

"Don't you see, you stupid bitch, they knew we were coming! What else do you think they know?"

"Oh, we always know when you're coming," came from Tracy, clearly enjoying herself, her glossy black hair shimmering in the downlighters as her head moved to and fro with her animated movements.

"You won't win, you sad fucks."

"Brandon, I won't tell you again. There are ladies here who would choose not to hear such expletives. One more and I am afraid I'll have to gag you. Now, what's it to be?" Griff then retrieved the roll of duct tape that had been there all along on the coffee table and used it to bind Brandon's arms to the back of the chair.

"Your sad, little security force won't win. You are swimming in a much bigger pond now to outsmart us."

"Well, we outsmarted you two, didn't we, so at least we made a start. It seems, old man, that you two chaps are a long way from home."

Griff seemed to delight in effecting a more clipped English accent than either he, or indeed Tracy, his partner, was used to.

"Anyway, as you said it's going to be a day or so. We may as well all settle down. Whist or dominoes anyone?"

Chapter XVI

Phoenix

Miss Clancy woke from yet another unnatural sleep. At least some of the tortured imagery that she encountered at such times was beginning to ease.

Sadly though, as the alcohol's influence began to wane, so did some of its protective effects. The most momentous of these were the return of her distressing memories that her confrontation with Roy had re-kindled – precisely those that alcohol had subdued. More than this, the words spoken by Margaret in all innocence, the day she'd paid her visit, were the ones that now tormented her the most: for she knew that not only would she be incapable of experiencing a normal loving relationship, but also that such a thing would be forever denied to her. Rather than creating a reason to stay, in making that visit as she'd dared to believe, such words had only re-affirmed the need for her to depart.

She drank a glass of cold water, using her left hand which continued to allow more stability than her right. She drank without spilling any of the liquid and, in a further positive, her retching had now subsided. She held out her right hand in front of her and spread her fingers as far as she was able. Although at least some of the tremors had subsided she looked upon it like an appendage that no longer belonged to her: one that she was not fully in control of. She found a couple of chocolate biscuits, that she had deliberately saved for the time that she had hoped her stomach was least likely to reject them. Having retained the glass of water she chewed on them slowly but successfully.

She looked at the small table that was strewn with empty gin bottles. Slowly but methodically she cleared the table of the objects that served as a reminder of a dark time and place that she was now vacating. She came across the present that Toby had left for her in what seemed like an age before. It was still wrapped. She slowly opened it, her fine movements being especially difficult for her to control. Eventually she came to a hinged flat cuboid box which she opened. There inside, gleaming in the available light was a gold chain. In the middle of which a loop had been mounted and suspended from the loop a further link on which was suspended a charm in solid gold. She looked at the image of a bird which she recognised to be a Phoenix. Her left hand gently lifted the mythical creature mounted on the chain as it sparkled back at her.

Chapter XVII

Shaped Charge Projectile

Toby had committed all his agents including the mobile back up force; everyone was now in service with little or no rest periods. It came down, as all recognised, simply, it was time to do or die.

Early the following morning, the scientists Crisk and Mellor got into their cars at a similar time for the journey to work. Two groups of North Koreans followed them closely, two to each car. What neither party was aware of were the Horizon agents who followed for a short distance, only for them to turn off while another car fell into line behind them. Such changes were made regularly until the scientists got to work. There the foreign agents simply waited until Crisk and Mellor were due to drive home. Today was to be the day that the full set of data would be available. As soon as they received it the interlopers were planning to kill everyone and make off with the information.

Once inside the power station and away from prying eyes, more Horizon agents met the scientists in the turbine hall. They informed them that the plan was to substitute false and useless data. Dr Crisk would not agree.

"Look, they are not just paid thugs, one or two of them have an idea of what they are looking for. Any attempt to bamboozle them could go badly, both for us and for our loved ones. Besides, we haven't the time to create credible but useless data."

Tomkins did not hesitate, and agreed with the scientists without demur. However, he immediately contacted Toby to inform him that the full data set would be leaving the plant that afternoon.

Horizon had bugged the North Koreans' cars. They were aware of the regular check-in signals that were made by short-wave radio to their colleagues who were holding the scientists' wives and Dr Mellor's children as hostage. Horizon reasoned that any attempt to strike at them could go badly for them all. For this reason, they decided to continue with the plan that was deemed to be the scenario most likely to succeed and minimise casualties.

Jenkins was working a continuous shift in the bunker and he'd been joined by one of the secretaries, Judy, who was not a field agent but knew how to work the surveillance and communications systems.

Judy was not an expert on the sophisticated displays but she knew by heart the security procedures that the operators were required to follow. Within seconds of her arrival, the night before, in line with current protocols, she'd reset the door access code, so that nobody could enter, and also the console activation code. Even the Horizon agents would have to have it given to them in order to gain access.

Judy rose from a couple of hours' sleep. She accepted that it was going to be a busy day. The Horizon forces were planning to secure the data and to protect the scientists and their families from harm and from the presence of the North Koreans. She'd been fully briefed and was aware that such things paled into insignificance beside the threat that confronted them all. She knew that whatever form such a threat was to take, she would either see it on their surveillance cameras or she would hear it on the chatter from the communications links between the agents. Sadly, she was not aware of the brutal nature of the threat and the fact that she would face this first-hand with disastrous consequences. Jenkins had been up through much of the night in constant communication with Toby. She ran a hand through her tousled hair and decided that her only strategy was to gather it behind and restrain it with a bobble so that it would at least not get in the way of the headset and microphone she used.

She spoke to Jenkins. "Tom, thanks for the couple of hours, why don't you get some sleep before the operation begins?"

Almost as soon as Jenkins moved his mouth to respond, her own mouth opened with suppressed horror as she looked at the screen just behind her colleague. She was drawn to the images that were displayed in the monitor showing the scene beyond the locked and reinforced steel door. She could see four men out there. More importantly, she could see that they were furiously typing in the four-digit access code.

One of the four men slammed his fist against the smooth, brushed-steel panel.

"Fuckers have changed the code!"

His colleague nodded to him, "No problem, Randy, good job we brought the gear with us," he nodded in turn at the black holdall that lay at their feet.

Jenkins looked as Judy gazed at the monitor with mounting panic. He chose his calmest most reassuring words and tone. "Don't worry, Judy, that's a reinforced steel door, they'll never get through it." He almost turned back to the main console to close his comms link so that she could take over when he noticed that she still remained transfixed by the images of the scene unfolding on the other side of the access door.

Judy was a secretary and had not received training on the use of either explosives or munitions. She had learned, as had all Horizon personnel, to fire a revolver, but very rarely chose to do so and she had not been in the shooting shed for some time. She certainly had no knowledge of the use of modern shaped charges. These had found widespread use in WW2 for destroying armoured vehicles and reinforced forts. The shaped charge, a relatively small device with a small amount of explosive, focussed intense kinetic energy on a specific area of the target and was able to breach even the thickest of armour plate. None of this was she aware of, but she knew they were under attack and she knew, despite the reassurances that Jenkins had provided her with, that they would get through that door and that it would be sooner rather than later.

She could see one of the four men, all of whom wore body armour and balaclavas, position something carefully against the steel door. The four faceless men worked in a well-co-ordinated flurry, as if they had done this many times before. In that moment she knew that she and Tom Jenkins now had only seconds of security remaining to them. She turned towards her colleague.

Jenkins heard her scream as the door failed. He grabbed his pistol from the rack under the console and Judy moved away from the door, as it blew inwards, to do the same. They were under the disadvantage of the weight of metal being blown violently towards them. Both of them reflexly tried to move out of its way and, by the time they had done so, it was already too late. Judy raised her forearm to her face in order to try to protect it from the blast as it came towards her. Their assailants had stepped back from the door as the shaped charges went off and also used hand-held shields to protect them. Then, in a perfectly co-ordinated move, two kneeling in the gap and two standing behind and above them, but all pointing automatic machine pistols, they stepped back to the gap as it formed, just before the door fell away, and sprayed the interior with bullets.

Both of the Horizon personnel received immediate, and ultimately, fatal injuries. Jenkins gifted perhaps a few seconds of life to Judy, as he stepped in front of her and took the full burst just as the door failed completely and came away.

Blood-soaked hands used these seconds as her vision was hampered by blood trickling down from a large cut on her scalp; by familiarity and touch alone she shouted into her microphone.

"Bunker's compromised. Repeat, bunker's compromised. Channel 2 to automatic, going dark. Goodbye, love you, Brady." She flicked the switch to ensure that communications were still available and then pressed a large red button in the middle of the console so that these settings would remain even as she died. More bullets hit her torso raking it violently.

As she fell to the floor, still gripping her microphone, she saw the icon 'MC1' appear on screen like a pulsating heart that she nearly didn't believe and almost didn't see, thinking this was nothing more than a delusion, perhaps at its most simple a dying person's last wish, but then, just before the vision in her blood-soaked eyes failed completely, she saw the graphic pulsate with a smooth and steady glow as the signal was locked on.

Somehow, in a last act of defiance, she managed to locate the long loop of chain coming from the control key that ran down from the edge of the communications console; it dangled in front of her as she went down. She pushed her right hand through the loop of chain so that it lay against her slender wrist, knowing only in the last second of her life that the weight of her dead body would pull the key from its socket.

Their attackers continued to fire into the Horizon personnel's now lifeless bodies as they rushed forwards. They avoided firing into the panels of surveillance and communication equipment. Just as they came forwards, however, and fifteen seconds after the key had been removed, the relays clicked over and the whole panel, together with all the screens and communications links, went blank as they shut down.

Seeing the consoles extinguish, one of the four-man attack team rushed forwards, grabbed the key and tried to reinsert it. One keyboard then glowed and a message came up. 'Enter security code to proceed, you have two attempts.'

Rocco, the man at the console, looked away from the uncooperative screens and down at the young woman's body on the floor, her eyes now staring wide having embraced untimely and violent death. "Limey bitch has shut the whole goddamned thing down."

Another of the men looked at the gold locket round her neck that had burst open; the picture of her husband lay floating in a pool of her blood that was already beginning to coagulate.

As one of the men sat at the console trying, but failing, to coax it back to life, two of the other men dragged the bodies into the corner to free up some room while the fourth man sent a signal. "Force Delta One, message to central, the comms console has been neutralised but is not functional." As the men sat there awaiting further instructions, a high-speed link had downloaded and transferred all the data to a remote server. As this information was received and stored, another fully-automated communications device came on-line to handle communications between Horizon agents.

All the Horizon agents paused as the message came through to them. They all knew who was in the bunker and also the full implication of that message. All the agents' thoughts in that moment turned to Brady.

Tim, looked at Brady. "Brady, I am so sorry; I didn't realise they would stoop so low as to attack the bunker."

Brady's fury knew no bounds, it outweighed even the unfathomable depth of sadness etched on his ghostly face, as he now stared off into a void in the middle distance that only he could see, and all others could only imagine. "We thought she'd be safe there. We thought even if they tried, they'd never get through that door. She was just a secretary, not even an agent and I can guess what these bastards did to her and Jenkins. That's what these bastards always do; shoot to kill. They don't know any other way. Jenkins was married with three young kids." There was a slight pause; Tim and the other agents could only stress how sorry they were. Brady continued, "When I get my hands on her, I will tear her limb from limb." Tim understood exactly what he meant but said nothing. He could only privately think how much he agreed with him.

Perhaps as a blessing to all present that day, Brady had no time to think and no time to grieve. Drs Crisk and Mellor left the power plant early, having secured the last of the data. The

North Koreans were waiting for each of them in order to accompany them home, while observing the Koreans, watching and waiting like grizzly bears looking for migrating salmon shooting the rapids in fast-flowing Canadian rivers, were the two teams from Horizon.

Dr Crisk arrived home at about 1pm. As soon as he entered the house, Janet appeared at the front door. She knocked loudly as if she were in some distress.

Mrs Crisk was sent to the door.

"Forgive me, my car's stranded down the road and my mobile has no charge, I couldn't use the phone could I?"

"Mrs Crisk thought quickly. No, I'm sorry, the landline is not working, nor is the mobile. Something to do with a fire in the exchange and work on the masts or something."

Janet pushed past her. "Well, do you mind if I at least try, it won't take a minute."

As soon as she gained entry, she entered the living room. At the same time another agent followed her, while two more burst through the back door.

A further two Horizon agents had captured and restrained two of the North Koreans outside the house. Janet saw that Dr Crisk was strapped to one of the dining chairs, his arms tied through the frame. Four North Korean agents were in the room. With no further ado Janet shot two of them and pointed her handgun menacingly at the remaining two.

Karen McCready was right behind Janet.

Mrs Crisk gave out a shriek of horror as the North Koreans fell, the blood spattered up the living room walls as the bullets passed right through them.

Karen was also shocked, "I thought we were supposed to capture and restrain the Koreans?"

"You can mess about if you want, Karen, I'm here to get the data and I think messing about with half measures is a good way to get killed."

"But they hadn't even drawn their weapons."

"No shit Sherlock? I don't have time for blowing smoke up their butts, I'm here to get a job done."

At this point two further agents came in from the kitchen, Wardle and Roberts.

"Bloody hell, Janet, it's like a bloodbath in here."

"More than you'll ever know, Wardle."

Suddenly, Janet moved behind Karen McCready and jabbed her Glock into her ribs.

"Drop your weapons, boys, and maybe we'll see a way to letting you live. Meet my real friends."

As Janet said this, four further agents entered the room, two at the front and two from the back. A further four were outside and had disarmed the two Horizon agents who had remained there.

"Janet! What's going on here? I take it you are not on our team?" Karen asked.

"No, not some loser limey team, I am part of the winning team and it's time for us to collect. All we want is the data and we will be on our way. No need for anyone to get hurt, but this is an option if you mess with me." She presented the Glock and stamped on their communicators one by one as she plucked them violently from their ears. "Now, where is the SSD?"

"Last minute change of plan, Janet. Dr Mellor took it home and, by now, Tim should have it."

"I doubt that, Karen, we sent a team there too, and if Tim is still alive he'll be singing like a canary, begging my colleagues to take it and spare his miserable life."

Suddenly, Janet barked out more orders, "Scoota, Frazer, you stay here and restrain all of them. Make sure that all their communicators have been destroyed. I am going to meet up with my ex and see if he's still gotta pulse."

She touched the pink Fitbit ever present on her left wrist, lifted her arm to bring it closer and spoke into it. "Zulu Niner, have you control of the situation there? Good, I'm on my way there now."

"Fancy device you have there, Janet." Offered Karen McCready as she nodded to what everyone had assumed for all this time was a simple Fitbit.

"State of the art, not like that shit you have," she looked at the crumpled communicators on the floor."

"They kept us ahead of you, Janet."

"No, don't think so, Karen."

While two of Janet's colleagues restrained the Horizon agents, Janet sped off making for Dr Mellor's house.

CHAPTER XVIII

Sea Trial

True to her word, Dame Helen had requested extra sea patrols out of Liverpool. These carried out surveillance sweeps for the whole of the Mersey estuary and much of the Irish Sea. High-definition radar had detected both the large submarine surfacing and the SS22, high speed attack boat much beloved of the marines, that was being launched as quickly and unobtrusively as possible. She had notified Toby immediately, even in an unheard of move using her personal phone to phone him and warn him.

"Toby Richmond."

"Ah, yes, Mr Richmond, it's Dame Helen here. I promised that I would let you know of any developments. As we anticipated, an attack boat has been released from a large submarine off the coast of Anglesey. I am going to send you the co-ordinates now. You don't have much time. By the time it has been cast off from the submarine, they'll load it and send it on its way directly. They won't want to be seen and as soon, as the boat has been launched, I suspect the submarine will submerge and await events."

"Thank you for this, Dame Helen. Yes the co-ordinates have come through now. I am on my way there now."

"Good luck, Mr Richmond."

"Thank you, Dame Helen."

Unbeknown to him, she'd also despatched covert observers who would monitor the situation and report back directly to her.

Toby had made good time. He was in position and ready to fire in less than thirty minutes.

Mercifully, he had not been that far away and after some precipitous driving he found himself approaching what was expected to be the embarkation point. He extracted his rifle from his boot and ran to take up position. He looked down his Schmidt and Bender sight, the type beloved by Clancy; how much better a job she would have made of this than he. Although, he realised, even she, when at her best, would have great difficulty landing such a shot on one of the engine cowlings at this range, at such a target speed and in such choppy water. He shook himself back to reality. Clancy was far away, and certainly in no position to even attempt any sort of precision shot or any shot at all, he reasoned. Such times were long gone and it would serve no purpose for him to reminisce in this way. Focussing his thoughts and his aim to the shot in hand, he could only hope that Clancy's influence was somehow with him that day. He calculated that taking out one of the two engines would cause the most disruption and delay to their visitors, who were now approaching as quickly, as the roar from the engines became more intrusive the nearer they came.

Toby wasn't a particularly religious person, and yet he was praying now. The SS22 high-speed attack boat was heading for the quayside at Cemaes bay. The craft was sweeping in now to pass the sea wall and soon the occupants would disembark. Even from this distance, he could see it was packed with Marines. Despite, or perhaps because of, the prodigious power from the engines, the boat continued to be tossed by the sea, despite its having entered the calming waters within the perimeter of the sea wall.

Upon making landfall, they'd disembark quickly, form a tight perimeter while they recovered their agent and then within seconds they'd warp out of the bay as quickly as the gas turbine engines could convey them. Toby estimated that their speed must be easily 50 knots and the twin turbines could be seen either side of the craft as it shot forward.

If only he could take out one of those engines, he'd buy enough time to frustrate their efforts completely. They'd then either have to be recovered or they'd have to escalate the whole mission into a full blown attack; something they could not later dismiss as a joint exercise that the government had known about and sanctioned.

Toby could not delay a second longer. He fired off a shot, suspecting that more would be required. Miracle of miracles, he saw the projectile hit the engine nacelle. His prayers had been answered and it was, without doubt, the best shot he'd ever mounted. His mouth fell open with wonderment and surprise. Catastrophically, however, the armour piercing shell bounced straight off with a spark given off by the fleeting metal on metal contact. The craft continued to approach; the roar from the gas turbines very much in evidence now as they were about to enter the bay. He could clearly see one or two of the marines pointing to their disembarkation zone. He could also see several trail bikes lashed to the decking plates.

He looked skywards; Toby recognised a fluke when he saw one. He would never be able to mount another shot like that one if he fired repeatedly for the next month. And yet, it was vital to keep them from making a landing. Things would turn very nasty if he allowed such a thing to happen and, for sure, he would be the first casualty. No doubt, the report later would confirm that somehow a live round had got into one of the visitors' assault rifles and by a catastrophe of bad luck this would have been the shot that had killed an innocent bystander. Their regrets would be staged to perfection and, meanwhile, they'd have completed their mission.

He prepared to shoot again, and he would go on shooting until either they'd killed him or he'd run out of bullets.

He was aware of something moving to his left. A high precision rifle was placed on its rest on the quayside wall next to him. He saw that it was an Accuracy International rifle almost like his, but which had been painstakingly and expertly modified. Not only had he seen that rifle before, but in the past few weeks the person who was usually behind that rifle butt had been constantly in his thoughts. Once again, he shook himself as if desperately trying to deliver himself from a waking dream, that showed what was aligned with his deepest desire in that moment rather than harsh reality.

He looked at the marksman, daring to witness the one person he hoped might be there.

"Clancy!"

"Another pickle you've got yourself in? I've only been gone for two minutes and here you are! Up to your handsome neck in it."

His face lit with a broad smile but, somehow, his mouth refused to do more than hang open as words in that moment failed. Tired eyes glowed with renewed vigour as they locked on her.

She, feeling the weight of his gaze, nodded towards the wind-tossed seascape. He moved to hug and kiss her. She shook her head. "Careful, this is a precision instrument, and the rifle's delicate too." He laughed, he could see her already preparing herself for the shot. The way her eyes narrowed, her brow furrowed, the way she caressed the stock of the rifle as her vision focussed on the target like an eagle soaring high above the terrain.

"Those nacelles are armoured, the AP bullets won't penetrate at this range. That's why your round bounced right off. And, might I add, that wasn't a bad shot for you, Toby."

"Well, somebody had to step up and do the precision work after you left."

She nodded in agreement as she acknowledged the difficult shot he'd made.

"So, if the engine housings are armoured, what are we going to do? What are *you* going to do?"

"I'm going to send them round in circles?"

"*How*, if those engines are armoured?"

"Can you see the inspection hatch on the side of the engine nacelle?"

"No, Clancy, I *can't* see that."

She handed him some binoculars. He thudded them against his eye sockets so quickly that the pain stunned him into a longer pause than he'd intended.

"Oh, yes, I can see it now."

"Good job I'm here, then"

"I'll never say or believe anything else, Clancy"

"That inspection hatch is made from mild steel, and I am going to put a shell right through it."

His words began, "But, but nobody could make that...," and then he realised if there was one person who could indeed make that impossible shot, at this range on a rapidly moving target, one that was being tossed by vigorous waves, this person was beside him. "Give 'em hell, Clancy."

She looked at the storm clouds, and the seagulls wheeling round the air currents. She felt the salty gusts of the wind as it stung her cheeks. Having assessed the situation, only then did she peer through her precision sight. Her eyes narrowed even more as they locked on her target. She breathed in, held her breath just for a second and then came the exhalation. As she did so the precision trigger was activated and the rifle fired. By all accounts from the witnesses who were present that day, the shot that Clancy made was one of the finest ever mounted – even by her standards. For sure Toby had seen her make some amazing shots that verged on the impossible and yet that day, as the bullet followed its trajectory, it almost had a charmed life. It must have taken almost a second for that shell to find its target. At the outset, if one had been able to follow that bullet as it made its scorching flight one would have thought that it could only be off-centre and markedly so. The wind, however, caught it on its trajectory just at the right moment. Furthermore, it was almost as if she'd compensated for rotation of the earth as well as its curve. Right on cue, the surging waves brought the attack boat up just to the right height as the screaming engines then delivered the boat, the engine and its inspection hatch, to now meet that specially-tipped shell with catastrophic effect for the force hoping to make land that day.

If any of the marines had realised that they were being fired upon they would still hold the conviction that even an accurate shot would neither pierce the hull, nor bring down the engines.

The AP round pierced the inspection hatch, which was no more than a foot square, and it continued directly on to encounter the vital and sensitive innermost workings of the turbine rotating with unquantifiable speed. Such was the roar from the air intakes, the thudding of the waves and the all-encompassing droning from the turbines that none of the occupants were aware, at first, that their craft had been fatally compromised. The first hint of the engine's distress came from the change of note. A high-pitched whine was given off and then a sound that Toby liked to refer to as an expensive noise, as turbine blades began to slice through each other at a speed and temperature that no man-made material could withstand; the highly-revving engine suffered catastrophic failure and destroyed itself within the two or three seconds that followed. Black smoke issued precipitously back through the air intake in an oily cloud.

The craft immediately felt the loss of the engine, which coughed and then exploded: the force of which, fortunately, was held within the confines of the engine casing. The boat, however, began to spin round as the other engine continued. The craft lurched violently and began to take in water as the bilge pumps were powered from this starboard turbine – the one that was now burning comprehensively. The helm could not respond to such a rapid and momentous change of forces acting upon the craft. Two of the marines wearing full body armour and helmets were tossed into the restless sea.

"Clancy, wow, I love you. He hugged her."

"Later, Toby; later, you can tell me how pleased you are to see me. I need to get Tim."

"Yes, Janet is en-route. She doesn't know we bugged the scientists' houses and she's on her way to Dr Mellor's house. I sent Tim and Brady in ahead of the schedule we released to all others so that, hopefully, Tim has secured the data. He'll be in the greatest danger."

"Can I leave you here? I need, need to…"

"Yes, yes, just go, Clancy. Dame Helen has launched a flotilla of naval protection vessels from Liverpool which will find the craft that has launched this pursuit boat and ask them if they have *accidentally* strayed into British waters. We suspect it's a bloody big submarine. *You go* and get Tim, Clancy. Also, you heard what happened in the bunker. If Brady gets his hands on her he'll rip her apart with his bare hands."

"If it wasn't so sad, I would pay money to see that," she said, her face riven with distress.

She grabbed her AI rifle and prepared to run back to her F-Type. Toby kept an eye on the pursuit vessel, which had now stopped completely, its stern having settled even lower in the water in those few seconds. It looked as though more than a few of those marines would either be baling for some time or they'd have to leave their equipment behind and swim for it. Through the binoculars, he could see that the steel locker that contained life vests was open and one of the marines was hastily distributing the contents while others hung over the coamings in order to help their drowning colleagues.

"I'll watch our cousins, you go."

"Oh and Clancy,"

"Yes?"

He kissed her forehead, like a father dropping his daughter off at the school prom, "So glad to have you back,"

"You only want me for my shooting."

"Oh no, Clancy, we want you for so much more than that. Oh, you know about the Mark 2 case?"

"Yes I've been monitoring your comms for a while. Good job I realised you'd switch to Channel 2, when you invoked the mission compromised protocol."

"Well, you drew it up, Clancy! Indeed, I am hoping that it has given us the edge. Oh and Clancy, don't forget these." Toby held out a tiny packet of ear protectors.

"Whoops, yes, thanks, Toby, I guess I will need them."

As Clancy ran towards her F-Type she heard him say that he hadn't had as much fun watching the spectacle before him since witnessing the clowns larking about at the circus, when he was a little boy. Rather like such a scene the marines were having trouble standing on the uneven deck that was both spinning and suffering extreme roll, pitch and yaw following the loss of the engine. Some were clinging to the side rails, some were vomiting as a result of the turbulence and several more, all in full body armour, were over the side and desperately trying to stay afloat under their weight of kit that each sported.

The rifle stowed in her car boot, Clancy fired the engine until it roared and the very ground seemed to tremble under the awesome power that was waiting to be unleashed.

Without further hesitation, the car shot from the bay and on to the coast road that led round to Bull Bay. She'd gone only a few hundred yards and felt her stomach intervene emphatically.

She stopped the car just in time and managed to open the door as she vomited uncontrollably. Even more catastrophically her right hand started shaking relentlessly and she knew that she would be unable to mount any shots even at close range until it had stopped. At times such as these her lesson lately had been a very simple one; just have another drink. She knew, however, that she'd parted with this for good and she wasn't going to return to it, even if it meant the loss of her life. She'd rather go out with her principles than lose them and survive. Clancy got back in the car and continued her journey, her grip on the wheel trembling so much that she had to assist her right hand with the left.

CHAPTER XIX

Last Woman Standing

Janet had arrived at Mellor's house within minutes; her mood far from happy. As she entered she found six Koreans who'd been disarmed and restrained. Four Horizon agents had also been disarmed and had restraints on their wrists behind their backs as they sat on the floor under the watchful gaze of two of Janet's colleagues. The fact that they'd all been restrained was the only thing that stopped her from shooting still others. One of her team met her as soon as she entered.

"What's your report, Travis?"

Travis coughed a little nervously; he knew she hated things going against them, "They *knew* we were coming; they arrived ahead of us; they must have known about us and about *you*, Janet. Wainwright already had the data; he says he's hidden it and only he knows where. He says we'll just have to shoot him."

"Then shoot the fucker," offered Janice as she raised her Glock in Tim's direction.

Tim was standing in the middle of the room. He held a gleaming case, forged from a single piece of elemental aluminium, in front of him defiantly.

Tim had left his communicator open. All the other agents could hear what was said.

Janet pointed her Glock at him.

"It's not at all like you, Tim, to come over so brave all of a sudden."

"I have news, Janet, I volunteered for this role, Toby wanted to do it."

"Well, looky looky, a genu-ine hero, if I ain't mistaken. A dead one soon enough. When did you know, Tim?"

"The *chips*. I reasoned it was such an unusual thing to just drop in a conversation unless you'd been privy to the conversation – the private conversation – during the mission in the Embassy."

"You clever fucker, Tim. You didn't think we'd just let you walk in, to the *American Embassy* for fuck's sake, and out again, did you? We were monitoring you the whole time."

"I know that now. I went through the video feeds and on one you are clearly seen talking to Mr Nukumobo. He was on the other side of the room, miles away, and didn't see a thing. He certainly couldn't have seen Miss Clancy shoot that waiter; he was simply too far away. You told him about us and you told him to approach us. You just wanted to know if we were capable of mounting serious missions and whether the Government were going to use us again. It was then that you appeared in the coffee shop and you just waited for your chance: one that we, one that I, gifted you. You just used me."

"Holy fuck, yes! Duh! Like it's news! Hello! And it worked like a dream. All we then had to do was get Clancy out of the way and that was easy too. Her taking on that paedophile guy and then fucking her own brains up was a really good thing for us. We guessed she's the only one with the cojones. Getting rid of her was our priority and it worked beyond our wildest dreams. We knew we'd never turn her. What could we offer a sad old fuck like her anyway? So, getting rid of her was a gift. I was told to pull you away using any means necessary and she would be history, and so she was. Don't look so hurt Tim, but you and me, seriously? Besides I'm sick and tired of you moaning Clancy's name in the middle of the night. We knew that sooner or later your snivelling underhand government would allocate you a proper mission, one with a bit of spine to it. I was in position, just waiting, and it came much sooner than we thought, though God knows how the North Koreans got on to it. Little did we realise we'd hit the jackpot. Anyways, time for me to move on as soon as I've got what I came for."

"Tim, I'm going to need that information. Where have you hidden it?"

"I'm afraid you're going to have to shoot me."

"We have your mom and dad. I just talk into my little fit bit here." She rubbed her wrist and looked at the fit bit that was always to be found there.

"So, that's how you were communicating with your *true* friends," Tim confirmed a little distastefully, "It won't do you any good, Janet, I think you'll find that 'Brandon' and 'Teresa' are being held by Griff and Tracy and, no doubt, all being entertained by my mother. Sadly, you weren't privy to the real operational orders that Toby gave out, on channel two. He just fed you what we wanted you to know on channel one!"

She paused, the lack of traffic that she'd monitored made sense now. "And, it's benefited you how, exactly? I still have the gun and you are the one about to receive a present from it. So, if you've all been so smart-ass, suppose then I just shoot you." She levelled her Glock in his direction; he knew the safety would be off.

"Don't think I won't, Tim, this is your last chance."

"I'm not going to tell you Janet. I am a small price to pay if we stop you, and we will stop you. It's all over, whether you shoot me or not. Shoot me now Janet, let's get on with it."

She swung the gun round.

"OK, I get it, wanna be all brave – but dead. I'll grant you your wish later. If you don't tell me and tell me *now*, then I'm gonna shoot the kids first then their mom. So, Tim, just how much is it worth to you? I'm gonna count to five and I fire on five.

Travis, go get one of the kids."

Travis barely hesitated, he moved towards the couple's daughter, shielded now by her mother. As he approached there were screams and illimitable begs and entreaties from both parents. They'd been promised by Horizon that they would be safe: all of them. A wail of sheer terror came from the two children, reflecting the sense of fear given off by their parents seconds before as their true fate sank in. Their mother was now sobbing as she pulled them ever closer to her. Travis used brute physical force to pull the daughter from her mother. The screaming and unending sobs from the whole family became even louder as one of the other agents intervened to stop Mrs Mellor from attempting to protect her child.

"One," Janet stared at him without blinking.

"Two,"

"OK, Janet, stop. Just don't shoot the kids. The SSD is in the case." He held the gleaming panels in front of him. Just as he did so he pulled the red spacer away from its socket and the case snapped shut.

The words, "Closing and sealed," came from the case.

"Not the bloody aluminium case! You stupid fucks, do you think your little sad fuck of a case is gonna stop the CIA from opening it?

Here, let's get it open straight away, shall we?"

One of her colleagues held Tim while another forced his fingers on to the chromed panels on top of the case.

"Negative, you have one more attempt or the contents will be destroyed," came the inanimate voice, once again.

"As you can see Janet, not just any case. You have one more go and if the incorrect fingerprint is used the whole contents are sprayed with twice molar Sulphuric Acid."

"You   think   our   tech   guys   can't   open   it?" "Actually, that's right, I think they can't. Our tech guys say that they can't. Why not try again Janet; let's see it do its stuff." She paused while she assimilated the new information and he continued, sensing she was on an ebb tide, "Then, of course, there is the X-Ray sensor and the vibration detector if you try to see what's inside or drill it – this too releases the acid."

"Loooky, loooky, here, just what I got! This is a key that opens everything." She brandished her Glock with the wild look in her eye that he'd seen so many times – just before she shot someone. She pointed the gun at him. "Tim, you tell me whose fingerprints will open the case or I will blow your brains all over that wall"

"Go ahead, Janet. I'm not afraid."

"Well Tim, you should be! So, wise guy, tell me now or one of the kids dies."

"Janet, I am sorry to tell you that not even I know. We wanted the situation safe, we wanted to either make the data safe or destroy it."

Janet nodded to one of her colleagues and then in the direction of Mellor's daughter. "Tie her hands behind her back and lash her to that kitchen chair. I reckon her brains being spattered on the walls will soon refresh Tim's memory."

Janet presented her Glock.

"Three."

"I may get bored and shoot before five, Tim and this will be on you. Tell me what I want to know and at least the kids live, though I am so pissed that I can't say the same for anyone else."

"Not the kids, Janet, this is between us adults, the kids are innocent."

"And you are the ones who put them in the middle of this. I fell for it too, thinking you'd send the data along with Crisk."

"We knew you'd swallow that, which is why we arranged for it to come here."

"Okay, enough talk; go and get the girl, and as soon as we have the data, then we take him," she nodded to the scientist, Dr Mellor, as his family wailed again as this unstable young woman raised their degree of terror yet another notch.

Suddenly a familiar voice appeared in the communicators over channel 1.

"CIA shooting children now, eh Janet. I suppose, at least they can't shoot back."

"Old Pen! Now you have really made my day."

"I hate to break it to you, Janet, but I believe you are five years older than I am, thirty-four if I am not mistaken?"

"What the fuck's that got to with it anyways?"

"Just setting the record straight, Janet."

"An age you'll never see, Clancy. I was just going to shoot these kids and then I'll shoot Tim here."

"Four,"

"You leave him alone, Janet, this fight's between you and me. You are always going on about how much better a shooter you are, here's your chance, Janet. Or are you chicken?"

"That's it, Clancy, you've just signed your own death warrant. What would you like as a eulogy at your sad little funeral, attended by, let's see now, that would be *nobody*, I guess. As soon as I've killed you I'll shoot the rest. I wondered if you'd manage to stagger back to get shot like the rest of them?"

"Here I am then, Janet, time to put up or shut up. Let's see how good you really are. I'm outside, Janet. I'm coming for you. Bring your Glock."

"With pleasure, Clancy, you'll be meeting it soon enough just before I blast you to hell."

Janet spoke to her colleagues. "Tie this lot up so they don't do anything stupid. Get on to Langley about that case. I'll be back as soon as I've shot that stupid bitch. Anybody moves then shoot them to hell."

"Time for you to face me, Janet, one to one just like you wanted. Here is your big chance to show everyone what a great shooter you are. I'll be there in a second or two and I can't let you shoot those kids or Tim."

"You'll be the first to die, you old fuck, and when I've got what I want I'll shoot 'em all and blame you as I slip away."

"Oh, don't count on it. We have blocked both bridges off the Island including the railway and there's a no-fly zone. I'm told the Internet has gone down."

"Where are you, Clancy?"

"I told you, I'm outside and I'm coming for you."

Janet screamed very loudly as she left the house. Such a display wasn't for anyone's attention but rather was an attempt to prepare herself for the face-off with Clancy. She knew that she performed better when a little angry – which was more or less her perpetual state. She ran outside still screaming. Clancy could be seen walking towards the cottage. Range was about 200m. Most experts believed the Glock to be accurate to 50m but not much more. Over this range, only a rifle could achieve consistent results. Many successful shots had been made by a Glock at well over 50m but such shots were either in calm conditions or simply came down to luck. Worse still, the significant onshore breeze had stepped up a notch or two and was now bordering on a gale. This could only have the effect of putting off any shooter and also creating considerable sideways drift; the more so the longer the projectile was in the air.

"Once you're dead, I'll get that information and I'll escape somehow. Don't think your little toy security force is going to stop me and, as for the Government, they are frightened of their own shadow these days. We'll just apologise for a training incident gone wrong and we'll actually do something with this technology."

"It's not yours, Janet, and I can't let you just take it."

"Your dead body is gonna stop me, eh, Clancy. You arrogant, limey bastards; anything you come up with you give away."

"And I'm sure we'll find a way of sharing with Uncle Sam. A few trident missiles for our submarines and I'm sure it will be all yours, but you are not going to take it; you'll wait until we are ready to share."

"You fuckers: everything of any value you gave away. The jet engine, you didn't file any fucking patents. The Megatron radar, you parcel up in a box and ship to the States and then a few years later you are buying radar equipment from us that we used your invention to make! You sad fuckers. The plane that broke the sound barrier was your plane, we just put our sticker on it. And then, you give away a complete Rolls-Royce jet engine to Stalin who reverse engineers it, then drops it by the thousand in Mig fighters and starts shooting our flyers down with it over Korea."

"I'm not saying we are always right, Janet."

"You are *never* right; you always do the dumb fuck thing. That's about all your sad little country is good at these days, the dumb fuck. *Special relationship*; it's a butt-end joke. We all laugh at it, and at you – all of you lousy limey Brits."

"Well then, that's our choice to make, as now, and that's why it's the end of the road for you, Janet. Give up now and most of you get to go home." Janet held her Glock in front of her using the two-handed grip to steady it against the wind. Clancy had not drawn her weapon, but she approached as the two women converged.

Janet's answer, as well as her intent, was to fire off the first shot, which drifted considerably to windward of Clancy. The howling wind strangely muted the shot as if a bullet of that calibre, at that speed, would not kill upon contact.

Clancy stepped sideways towards the direction of the bullet, which was to her right, but as she did so she continued to walk; the gap was closing.

Janet's second shot was off to Clancy's left and she continued down the hill. On this occasion, Clancy moved to her left.

"Once you are dead…" As she spoke, Janet had hit upon an idea: her Glock was slightly longer-barrelled and it would take a clip-on laser sight. "I'm gonna seize that technology. Uncle Sam will use it and we'll have it in mass production by the time of your small insignificant funeral at which there'll only be Toby, that's if I don't shoot him if he comes anywhere near here."

The communicator clicked in once again. "I'll be right there, Janet, just finishing watching what's left of your attack boat. It's well down in the water and I don't think it will be afloat for much longer, then you can have your shot at me. It's going round and round in ever-decreasing circles, heading straight for the bottom of Cemaes bay; all the marines are getting sea sick. Seems someone shot out one of those engines through an inspection panel. They say it was one hell of a shot. So, I'm thinking that the only way out for you is that high speed pursuit boat that is going nowhere, apart from sinking that is. I bet those friends of yours are getting very dizzy. Most of the trail bikes have gone off the side to keep the boat afloat"

"As soon as I've blasted Clancy to hell, then you can be next, Toby"

"I'm on my way, in that case, Janet."

Clancy's Glock was a more compact model that would not take a rail to mount the laser direction sight that Janet proceeded to clip on as she continued to speak, temporarily stopping her walk as she did so.

"It's over, Janet, we were way ahead of you, thanks to Tim. We outmanoeuvred you at every turn. Give up before more get killed."

"I'll get away, I'll be on my way to Langley by tonight at the latest. You Brits will do nothing apart from come crawling to us like a puppy that's been beaten by its master."

"No, I don't think so Janet, can't see you making that attack boat, or that submarine. It seems that there's a fishery protection exercise going on with lots of boats and one or two destroyers coursing up and down. I think it'll be a while before that sub can surface, not that you've got any means of getting out there anyway. "

Janet fired again, the shot still wildly out.

"Hoping to get lucky Janet? Toby's on his way; there's no way out for you or your team.

Surrender now, you'll be deported and you'll live to fight another day."

"No, Clancy, you are going down big time."

Suddenly, she'd activated the laser sight. A red dot appeared in the centre of Clancy's chest as the laser found its target. The fine beam shimmered just a little but otherwise did not move from its target as it sparkled like a ruby: clear but deadly. Janet knew that this was to be Clancy's last move. Somehow she'd always known that this moment would come. The bullet would surely follow any second now. Janet squeezed the trigger and the kill shot was on its way. Laser light was unaffected by even strong wind but the bullet was not so immune and being caught up in it, it was swept wide. Janet's grisly smile was likewise swept from her face in the split-second journey time only for the bullet to whizz past Clancy.

"Nasty thing, this wind, Janet. I reckon it's stronger than it looks. Shame you've not got your Barrett rifle and your shot fall calculator and your windage compensator. Oops, what a shame you can't use them all at once and when the wind is blowing in gusts like today. What a shame that rifle is so heavy you'd have to put it on a rest to loose off a shot."

In addition to being slightly longer then Clancy's, Janet's Glock was also heavier. At first this was an advantage in the gusts of wind but, very soon, with its being held constantly in front of her while she walked and fired, its extra weight began to be felt. Clancy had not even drawn her gun but she continued to come closer.

"Give up, Janet, and you'll be back in Virginia in no time."

"Not until I've killed you."

"Then kill me, Janet! I hear the talk but what about the walk?"

Clancy now held her arms wide apart making the target even easier for Janet. Her next bullet was very close.

"You'll see the walk all right, it'll be over your dead body, while I dance on your unmarked grave."

Only then did Clancy draw her weapon and unlock it.

"Don't make me kill you, Janet?" She presented her weapon.

Janet was wearing a bullet-proof vest which left Clancy the choice of either a head shot or a leg shot, which might only disable her and still allow Janet to fire. Clancy knew that the former was the only option for her to be safe: to end it once and for all.

"Don't let it end this way, Janet."

"You useless fucker, you can't be certain of hitting *anything.*"

Clancy stopped, presented her Glock and crouched just a little. She kept both eyes fully open rather than attempt to look with just one staring down the barrel. In so doing, this gave her vital stereoscopic vision so useful for assessing distance to a given target.

She breathed in slowly and then began the long exhalation; as she did so she brought the barrel down ever so slightly and moved its traverse to compensate for the wind; timing it just as the gust abated.

Clancy fired twice in rapid succession. Janet fell within the space of that second. She'd been hit in both thighs the one in the right leg had grazed the thigh bone and severed the femoral artery causing profuse bleeding and intense pain. She gave off a laboured, gasping sound as the effect of the deluge of pain caused the breath to leave her body.

Clancy ran towards her and picked up her gun with the laser sight still attached. "Funny thing, Janet, all this gear still doesn't put a shot where you think it will. Better keep practising."

Clancy pressed her communicator.

"Emergency Ambulance to my co-ordinates." Clancy removed her belt and used it as a tourniquet to stem the profuse bleeding that was now issuing from one of Janet's legs. The CIA agent was still intent on shouting invective at Clancy but suddenly her strength evaporated as the blood loss began to tell and hypovolaemic shock set in. Even sitting up was now impossible and she lay flat, in an attempt to stop herself from passing out.

Clancy was aware that there wasn't much time. She knew that Tim and the other Horizon agents were still being held hostage, and with Janet being removed from the picture she wasn't sure how the others would take it.

Ultimately, all she could do was to support the plan that she knew Tim and Toby had formulated.

She got to the house. One of the CIA agents met her at the door and relieved her of her Glock.

"Where's Janet?" was his simple challenge.

"Waiting for an ambulance, that is on its way."

Tim was in the middle of the room sitting on a dining chair.

Behind him and in front of him were six CIA agents.

The six North Koreans had all had their hands restrained with plastic ties behind their backs and looked very miserable. They realised that, having stumbled across the information, the Americans were now intent on stealing it from the British and, also, under their noses. In many ways it looked as though they were now an irrelevance. No doubt the American agents would be victorious; for sure nobody could stand up to them, certainly not the British, who seemed to lose or disseminate every technological advance they had ever made. It was unlikely that the Americans, having taken control of the situation, would kill them. Certainly, the chances of this had gone down since that angry woman had been removed. More than one of the agents took the view that a noble death, perhaps it could even be stretched to 'killed in action', would be preferable to any of the alternatives. Even more than fearing for their lives, they realised that to return home to Pyongyang without success would go badly for each and every one of them and also for their families. They hoped that the British would take matters into their own hands and act decisively. By any analysis, they each realised that life in a British jail would be infinitely preferable to facing their unstable and vicious political masters. At the very best they would all spend the rest of their days in a work camp, where they would be slowly ground to dry, inanimate dust. They could only hope that the British would not try to strike a deal with their superiors. That's if the British were still around once the Americans had had their way. For sure the CIA seemed to have the upper hand and control of the situation. The girl that had just been brought in would be unlikely to change that.

Mellor, his wife and two children were similarly restrained with cable ties, and were strapped to the small kitchen table in the through room. The other three Horizon agents were sitting on the floor with their hands all tied behind their backs.

Agent Travis had assumed control in Janet's absence. The American was both tall and stocky. His pale but cold eyes surveyed the scene.

"Right, it's very simple. We want that data and we want it now. Let us have it and everybody lives. Refuse and one by one you all die, simple. Who wants to go first?"

Tim stood up, still clutching the case.

"Make any attempt to open it and the contents get frazzled. You'll never make it off the island with a hostage."

"Maybe, we are going to have to see about that. You mean you've been sent in here without the knowledge or the means to open that case."

"Exactly."

"Hand over the case and I'll get some images to Langley."

"I can open the case," offered Clancy, like a bomb going off in the room. All eyes were now locked upon her.

"Then do so, or we will start shooting."

The emergency claxon of an ambulance could be heard in the distance.

"Don't do it, Miss Clancy, the contents are safe and either protected or will be destroyed. Don't show them how to open the case."

"Tim, I have to, I can't let innocent people die and you know what they are capable of; they will kill everyone and still find a way of making off with the case."

"Also, we can't let them die," she nodded towards the children and their mother, all of whom were quietly sobbing, "or expose them to the horrors of what we know the CIA to be capable of when they want something." She stood facing Tim and held her arms forwards towards the case. "Just one second."

"Miss Clancy, they will kill us as soon as you have opened it. Let's end it now, the data will be destroyed, they'll never get away with a hostage in tow."

"Can we, do you think you could close the kitchen door? I don't want those kids to see if things go bad."

"Why should they go bad if you are so confident?"

"Look, this is not something that those kids should be witnessing. They have been through enough already. Please, then I'll open the case."

The CIA agent looked uncompromisingly at her, "You are in no position to dictate terms," and then, at the last minute, he nodded to his colleague who closed the kitchen door.

"This is your last chance; next, I start shooting." insisted the CIA agent whose pale but blotchy skin had now become more uniformly livid.

"In that case, Miss Clancy, I need you to know something, something really important," began Tim.

"Shh Tim, it's okay. There'll be time for you to tell me later." Her eyes sparkled like crystals of pure Muscovado, holding the promise of a new day to come and many more to follow − perhaps. "Trust me, Tim, I know all about the case." She nodded to him almost imperceptibly.

Gently, ever so gently, she took the case from him. She looked at her fellow agents who were in turn looking at her expectantly. Brady looked dreadful. He was well into the second phase of the bereavement reaction. First came disbelief, and now he was well into needing someone to blame. Such a thing seemed obvious, given the circumstances.

Clancy stroked the top of the case three times, her thumbs simultaneously making a sweeping movement outward as she did so.

Suddenly, two flaps opened on either side of the case. Upon hearing the clicking and slight whirring as the case gave up its contents, the CIA agents were ecstatic. Not for the first time would they be victorious, and it would be a simple matter of then getting off the island. The case gave off a slight clicking noise which was followed almost immediately by an unusual 'phutting' noise.

It was at this point that the CIA agents realised that they had been deceived and it was already far too late for them to effect a recovery. How could they have failed to notice that all the Horizon agents had moulded ear plugs in place. Stun grenades were ejected precipitously, one from each side, as the explosive air triggers activated. Below the case, a further flap opened to present a compact Glock, identical to the one the Horizon agents all received training on.

The stun grenades exploded immediately. The mixture of Magnesium and Ammonium Nitrate produced not only a debilitating noise of over 170 Decibels, but also a blinding flash of several million candelas. Clancy closed her eyes for a second as the flash went off. Recovering quickly, courtesy of the ear plugs that she'd inserted into her ears, she grabbed the Glock and immediately shot each of the three agents behind her in the shoulder, shattering their arm bones as she did so.

Tim grabbed the aluminium case and lashed out at the agents who were standing behind him.

Brady got to his feet and, although his hands were restrained, he used his long legs to kick the revolver from the agent closest to him.

Clancy, in turn, had used the body of the CIA leader whom she'd shot in the shoulder as a human shield.

One of the agents grabbed Tim from behind and produced a flick knife, which he held at Tim's throat.

"Put down your gun or handsome, here, gets slashed across the neck." His voice much louder than usual, his hearing having been affected. His ears were streaming blood from the ruptured tympanic membranes as were those of the other CIA agents.

Clancy spoke. "Are you sure you want to do that? It's all over here, you'll all live to fight another day. We aren't going to let you take what's not yours, full stop, so you'll just have to move on."

"Drop your gun, limey bitch, or I will slash him from ear to ear."

He'd grabbed Tim and had poised the knife ready to slash Tim. However, his footing was a little unstable and he wasn't quite ready to act. Nor was he counting on Clancy responding and without hesitation.

"Don't worry about me, Miss Clancy, just shoot him."

"Oh, no, Tim, we can't have you…"

Clancy fired immediately, long before she'd completed the sentence; the round sped past Tim's right ear and entered the CIA agent's right temple where there was an imperceptible delay as it pierced the skull and carried on through his brain making a large exit hole as it did so.

He was dead long before he hit the floor and Clancy had now unequivocally taken charge of the situation.

"Tim, use his knife to free Brady, Grant and Tomkins. Use the spare ties to restrain the CIA agents. I can hear the ambulance. I guess the police should be here any minute. Keep those kids out of this room, we don't want them seeing what's gone on in here. Are you all right, Tim? I am sorry I couldn't give you any warning. There was a sudden angle of fire opening up, so I took it."

"No, don't worry about me, Miss Clancy, thanks to you it looks as though we've carried the day."

"How did you know about the case?"

"Oh, it's something Toby and I worked on before I left. I had been monitoring comms on channel two. It seems that Janet was fed chatter and static on channel one while Toby gave out his real strategy on channel two and using the Blackberrys."

"I could tell you knew something when I saw you had ear plugs in, so I figured you knew the case contained stun grenades and the compact Glock."

"Where's the SSD, Tim?"

"I have it right here." Tim reached for his back pocket and withdrew the slim device. As you can see I just bluffed about its being in the case." He smiled as he held it up.

"Well done, Tim, excellent work, it seems we'll make an agent out of you yet."

"I live in hope Miss C."

She laughed, the first time in some months she'd done so.

Brady charged out of the house; Clancy knew where he was going. He was ready to confront Janet and, in his current state, she wondered if he'd simply gun her down without hesitation. She raced after him.

Brady came rushing out of the house and stood towering over Janet who was lying in considerable pain on the ground. He levelled his assault rifle at her. The paramedic and ambulance crew had drawn up and were preparing to transfer her onto the stretcher.

He screamed at Janet, waving his rifle in her direction as he did so, "It's on you, Janet. It's your fault she's dead. You knew she wasn't an agent. That's what the CIA do, gun everyone down, no-one matters to them. You lying, double-dealing bitch." Brady's hands were shaking so much that Clancy wondered if he might squeeze the trigger almost by accident.

"Go on then, Brady, finish it. You know you want to," gasped Janet between rapid breaths caused by the pain and the blood loss.

Clancy advised him, using the most soothing tones she could manage, "Don't, Brady, it won't bring Judy back, and don't give her the satisfaction. She'll bear those scars forever. We'll get justice for Judy in another way, I promise, but gunning Janet down is not the way to get that for her."

"It's all your fault, Janet, you treacherous bitch. Clancy should have put a couple through your forehead. That's what you deserve. She's better than you, Janet, a million times so, you're not fit to lick her boots, nor ours."

The ambulance crew had backed off fearing that bullets were about to issue incontinently from Brady's gun and that once begun they would go everywhere and would not stop until he'd exhausted the magazine.

"Brady, don't, don't do this; as you say, you are better than that, and better than her."

He nodded to Janet, "You are alive this time only because of Miss Clancy. If I ever see you again, then I will shoot you where you stand. Wherever you go, make sure you look behind you cos I'll shoot you in the back without warning, and that's what you deserve, consider yourself on notice."

The Police and ambulance appeared just as Toby arrived and the Horizon team melted away. They escorted Dr Mellor and his family away from the scene and Tim went to make sure that the force detailed to liberate Dr and Mrs Crisk had succeeded.

Nobody had seen a little old man sitting calmly on a bench facing the bungalow the whole time. As soon as the agents had gone and the CIA were in the process of being removed by the Police and ambulance, he clicked a small hand-held device. He touched it to his left ear.

"Observer one here, Ma'am. It seems the Horizon team came through better than we hoped. You can stand down the security forces now, Ma'am, it's finished. Your contingency plans won't be needed. It was a highly professional mission and, although several CIA operatives are wounded, there has only been one fatality. Observer two reports two North Koreans believed killed at Dr Crisk's house. And you were right, Ma'am, I've never seen anyone shoot as well as Miss Clancy."

Clancy had walked back up the road with Toby.

"Oh, Penny, another close call. Thank you, Penny, we could not have done it without you."

"Although, Toby, seems you were doing really well without me."

"No, I mean it. I told you we can't do this without you; I hope you're going to stay?"

"Well, that depends?"

"On what, just name it?"

"Well, whether you'll have me back?"

"Clancy, yes, yes a hundred times *yes*, just *please* don't go away again."

Chapter XX

Sine Qua Non

A few days later Toby pressed the 'activate' button on the secure link to Dame Helen. Her smiling face, an unusual thing in itself, appeared on screen.

Before she spoke, Toby said, "I hope you don't mind, Dame Helen, but I have Miss Clancy here with me?"

"So I see, Mr Richmond, and I am delighted to see *you*, Miss Clancy. I am told you returned just in time."

"You are too kind, Ma'am, but I am sure you will believe me when I tell you that things were well advanced, courtesy of the brilliant and unstinting efforts of my colleague here, who, as you know, overturned overwhelming odds to settle things in our favour."

"Yes, yes, of course, I was just coming on to that, if I might congratulate you, Mr Richmond, on a superlative mission. The cold-fusion plant came on-line two days ago and the power output far exceeds our boffins' expectations. It was kind of you to remove their families to your yacht, which, I believe, is making for Limassol."

"Thank you, Dame Helen. We are pleased that it was carried out to your complete satisfaction with a favourable outcome to HM Government and to the nation as a whole. As for the Crisks and the Mellors, they are cruising in the eastern Med as we speak. I thought it was the least I could do after what they'd been through. I am pleased the powerplant has delivered on its promise."

"Yes, quite so. A successful mission, there can be no doubt. We have so much work lined up for you."

"It's gratifying to learn that, Ma'am." There was more; so much more, like water piling behind a dam that was about to burst; suddenly it began to give way. Only the slight pause gave warning of what was about to flow. He knew that she didn't take kindly to not being allowed to spout forth. "Dame Helen, if you'll permit me, there is something of the greatest urgency that we must discuss with you." Normally such words would irritate her unfailingly, but something about the finesse and outcome of the mission, which could have gone badly awry, with limitless embarrassment to her government, meant that she could allow him some latitude. Her light-hearted mood even allowed for a return smile, for now, as he began.

"Well, in that case, Mr Richmond, you'd better tell me. What's on your mind?"

"The four Special Ops force that attacked our offices?"

Her smile vanished like igniting coils of magnesium, "Yes, Mr Richmond, a regrettable incident. I am truly sorry to learn of the loss of agent Jenkins and secretary Judy Brady. The men responsible are due to be deported."

"Ma'am, we would very much like them to stand trial," Clancy said firmly, a steely gaze of her own now fixed on the screen as she spoke. Dame Helen knew then why Clancy had asked to be included in the call that was normally one-to-one.

"Out of the question, Mr Richmond." Dame Helen hoped to ignore Clancy, and her words; by addressing herself to Toby she hoped to re-exert her absolute authority. "HM Government cannot afford any such exposure. We are in delicate negotiations with the Americans over, over, other matters and we cannot afford for these to be compromised. They will take very badly to their operatives being brought to book in this way. I'm afraid you'll just have to bear that loss, sad though it remains."

"Forgive us, Ma'am; we thought that would be the official line." came from the voice that Dame Helen was studiously avoiding. "You must forgive my directness, Ma'am, but we feel strongly that either these men should be tried in an open court, or we should be given leave to take matters into our own hands." Dame Helen nearly coughed at this impertinence; only a slight glimmer of sweat on her forehead belied more human considerations: ones that she wiped immediately.

"Out of the question!" She almost shouted dismissively.

"Now, shall we move on to your next assignment?" She had given her answer, and now expected things would move on quickly.

Toby shook his head with a finality that assured her that feelings had neither been assuaged, nor bypassed, "Forgive me, Minister, but all at Horizon are of the mind that we shall be unable to do so until this matter is resolved."

"*And* I've told you, Mr Richmond that these are my *instructions*." There was even more of a stiff formality now in her demeanour, like a teacher exerting discipline on an unruly class. "Now, we move on."

"I think, Dame Helen, that what Mr Richmond is saying is that none of us is prepared to move on until this matter has been settled. We lost, as you know, an experienced agent and Brady's wife under the most brutal of circumstances. If we had not had advanced warning, many more would have died."

Only now did she look, albeit incredulously, at Clancy and acknowledge her words, "Are you seriously telling me that you would give up future projects out of pure revenge?"

"No, Ma'am, but, without doubt, we would in pursuit of justice. Surely you would expect no less?"

"You have taken losses before."

Toby's calm manner remained but his voice found its deepest register as he summarised their position and their incontrovertible stance, "Indeed we have, Ma'am, but these two were killed needlessly, and almost as if they didn't matter. We need to signal that they mattered a great deal and seeking justice is the way to do this."

This was the dividend of success and also its price. Horizon had risked everything and completed their mission without hesitation or even pre-condition – until now.

Ultimately, Dame Helen was a politician, and minor considerations such as justice came quite a long way down her emotional lexicon; certainly a long way below political influence, self-advancement and self-preservation. She sensed that one or more of these was in danger now, given the recognition that Horizon had achieved and the lofty corridors of power in which their name had been whispered. In any event, she wasn't used to having, nor was she prepared to accept, her authority being challenged by people who were *paid* to do a *job*. She was about to learn much.

Toby delivered an ultimatum of his own, "We are of one mind, Ma'am, that if we cannot apply, or be seen to have applied, justice then we would humbly tender our resignation."

"And how many of you does this *resignation* apply to?"

"Why, all of us, Ma'am," came from Clancy, who was genuinely surprised as to how the Minister could not have assumed that feelings ran so high and were all-pervading.

"Indeed, I have never been so insulted," was the stock reply she sought refuge in now. "I am not used to being blackmailed in this way."

"There is no such intention on our part, Ma'am, but there is a need for closure for the whole team. Anything less would see multiple resignations on my desk and, to be truthful, I could not blame them: any of them."

The shimmer of perspiration on her forehead had now turned to a glow, the colour of bright puce. She decided to play for time and see from her superiors how much wiggle room there was on their request.

"Very well, I shall give you my answer in one hour and my decision shall be final."

As is the way with such things, neither Toby nor Clancy was prepared to back down. Their only surprise was that the politician could not see how strongly they felt about their request, which had long since become an ultimatum. They both concluded, however, without hesitating that a little tolerance, allowing the woman to save face, was a wise move.

CHAPTER XXI

Payment in Kind

The following day, in the late evening, a US transport plane took off from Lakenheath and set a course for Virginia, USA. The massive aircraft carried just four personnel of an elite black ops team whose existence was never acknowledged outside CIA circles. The highly-trained personnel had laughed and joked as they'd boarded but were relieved, nevertheless, at being extracted from a potentially sticky situation, returning home and then moving on to other discreet and high-level missions. They knew that Uncle Sam would protect them just as he always had and always would, no matter how badly things turned out or how high the body count. It was said that the British were jumping up and down; that there'd been talks and even a bit of table thumping at the highest level.

Ultimately, they knew that the Brits would back down, which they had, just as they always did. It was time for home; until next time, when, if need be, they'd do it all again and by whatever methods were required of them to get the job done.

Randy turned to Mitch, who had occupied the window seat. "Knew the limeys would back down, just who'd they think they are? Wanting to try *us* for God's sake, treacherous bastards, what are they trying to pull?"

"Right on Randy, Brits are scared of their own shadow these days, ever since we chopped them off at the knees over Suez. Have hardly heard a peep out of them since."

Rocco turned round from the seat in front, looking at Mitch, "Suez! What the fuck is that? Way before my time."

"Sure, their cocky Prime Minister thought he was going to kick some ass in Egypt over a little stretch of water that the Brits thought they owned. Until Uncle Sam reminded them those days are long gone. No, Siree, wan't gonna happun."

All four men laughed a little and soon settled to their specially-scheduled flight.

The lumbering craft banked a little and then set upon its westward-bound course. A formation of Typhoon jets passed them at speed and in tight formation. The distance was so small however as to allow, just before the light faded, each of the RAF pilots to form a salute to the two American pilots as they did so.

TJ pointed through the window just to his right. "Hell, the Brits are even providing a farewell salute. They know who's got the upper hand here. Just as well they know their place, guys."

The Typhoons sped away, still in rigid formation. Some time later, while the aircraft was well over the Atlantic, an engine warning light came on and the pilots announced that they would have to turn back. The nearest airfield which could accommodate the military transport, was East Midlands, there not being enough time to return to Lakenheath. The military aircraft banked sharply to effect the turn but just in time, as a fire began in one of the port engines. The four men sat staring at the flames, made much more prominent by the rapidly-fading light as the sun dipped below their horizon. The fire extinguishing system cut in immediately and just as the engine died the auto-feathering set the propeller blades parallel with the airstream so as to minimise drag. The three other piston radial engines took up the burden and the pilots were relieved that they were soon beginning their descent. The pilot informed them that Lakenheath was too far, given the nature of the fire, and clearance for landing had been granted at East Midlands airport.

Some time later, having been painstakingly coaxed by the pilots, the aircraft came to a stop on a remote part of the runway. This was deserted at this time, in the early hours of the morning. A gangway clanged against the outside of the metal fuselage, but the door did not open. The interior lights then came on and, after sitting there for a few seconds, the party of four decided to grab their equipment, open the door and vacate the plane.

It was only when charges blew the door, which was then opened to the total darkness outside the plane, that they realised that they'd soon be in a fight to the death. Their training kicked in at once and they quickly grabbed their sidearms and took up a formation designed to deal with whoever came through the door.

They primed their weapons in readiness – and then the interior lights went out.

There were one or two flashes in the darkness, but these were simply their own weapons as they were discharged against an unseen and unknown foe. The flare created by each shot gave away their position, a second later came the terminal scream of one of their members, Mitch, who was nearest the door, and then came silence. One of the men, Randy, grabbed a mobile phone and used this to illuminate the interior, but all he saw was Mitch's body, covered in blood and lying on the deck of the aircraft. Unfortunately for the three remaining, the mobile phone gave away their position, and by the time the mobile hit the metal decking of the aircraft, Randy, too, was dead. The attacker had faced a simple choice. A slash to the neck, severing the carotid artery, would be very quick but would cause blood to fly everywhere and coat the deck, in particular, with copious amounts of the Special Forces operative's blood. This would also make the decking plates slippery and the people who came through the door knew that their attack depended on both speed and certainty of all their movements. A stab directly at the heart was cleaner from this point of view, and almost as quick as the blade applied across the neck, but his attacker rejected this too. The blade, sharp though it was, could be slowed and fouled by the rib cage and would also give rise to typical grooves showing in the rib cage when his body was found later.

The attacker elected for a more complex thrust, where the slim blade was applied in an upward arc under the left lower rib, piercing the spleen and stomach but terminating in the heart, which would suffer catastrophic blood loss and failure as soon as the blade was removed. Most of the blood would be retained within the victim's body cavity. The disadvantage of this approach was that it required significant strength from the assailant in order to drive the blade as far as it needed to go, with the required speed. Strength, however, was by no means in short supply as anger, and determination to set scores right, conflated with lots of other emotions.

The illumination from the mobile phone remained for a few seconds as it lay upwards on the metal decking but it only served to display in gory detail the lifeless body of their colleague as it slumped downwards, to follow the mobile phone.

The two remaining shouted, screamed and cursed, while firing indiscriminately inside the confines of the cabin, seeing nothing but their two dead colleagues, now both slumped on the floor. TJ had exhausted his clip of bullets, and only then did he see his assailant, who had pulled herself up into the upper part of the fuselage, using the luggage racks as a purchase. She moved so swiftly that he was barely able to contemplate what fate awaited him. He didn't see one of her legs come forward to sweep his right leg from beneath him. As he stumbled, she caught him and spun him round so that she was now behind him. Rocco, who was in front of him, heard TJ scream just as the honed blade sliced through his neck, the blood now projecting forwards violently to cover Rocco with the gooey liquid, which was still warm and covered him completely.

Rocco had managed to reload and he fired in TJ's direction but his lifeless body absorbed nearly all of the kinetic energy from the bullets and the few that passed through TJ's body were deflected, even at this close range, by the bullet-proof vest she wore.

Rocco's gun was now, once again, empty and he was aware of a larger man brushing past the woman and past TJ's riddled and lifeless body, which was now allowed to fall to join his two other colleagues.

The last remaining member of the elite force begged and pleaded for mercy even as he fired his last bullet. He was aware of the silence as his words ran out. Only then did he become aware of massive hands applied to his jaw, and the blade that transected Rocco's windpipe didn't even provide for a terminal scream, as the hands were released and he slumped to the floor, dying a few seconds later from lack of oxygen. Just before this, as the massive hands with a vice-like grip twisted round to break his neck, he heard the words, 'Mercy, like you showed them?"

Only now did the light appear as the two attackers lit a fuse for a petrol-filled plastic flask, which was then tossed into the plane as they made their escape down the gangway.

The large man said to the woman, "Thank you, thank you for coming with me. She would have wanted you to make sure I was all right."

"And I always will, I promise; I won't leave again."

She moved to hug her colleague and his strong arms and sizeable hands pulled her slim but muscular form towards him. He caught the delightful smell that her hair gave off as he brushed against it but it only served to remind him of all that had been lost.

Just as they started to descend the steps the woman stopped as if making to head back.

"Whoops, I forgot, I promised not to damage the plane."

He looked behind them as the flames licked up, "Bit late for that," he laughed, as the blaze caught hold and searched relentlessly for the still brimming fuel tanks.

An electric golf buggy, which had no lights, waited for them at the foot of the gangway and seconds after boarding it they sped away to the edge of the airfield, where an open security gate allowed them to exit and find their cars, which were parked nearby.

Chapter XXII

No Cloak No Dagger

Two people walked side by side along the old dockside at Salford Quays. It was late and the walkways were deserted. The ghosts of the old steamships that had plied the North Atlantic were the only things to bear witness. The pubs, restaurants and cafes had emptied and had either closed or were about to do so. The miserable few who'd drawn the late shifts were hurriedly mopping floors and wiping tables, so that the numerous businesses could open promptly the following day. The TV studios, that had replaced the warehouses and cranes, remained at least partly lit, as the late-night news and sports teams still had to give their final updates for the day.

The couple walked in the opposite direction from the bars and studios and, although there were one or two illuminated navigation lights along the waterways and bridges, the dense cloud had blotted out the full moon, which had shone in its reflected glory, some hours before. For much of the time, as was her wont, they'd strolled in complete silence. They'd travelled this way and this route many times before, he closest the water, as always, and she to his right. On this particular night, however, something was different.

Perhaps it was the clear night air, punctuated only by the gentle lapping of the water on the dock sides, or even the dark clouds sliding by the golden hunter's moon that bathed them, periodically but briefly, in its bewitching light. Perhaps it was the unusually warm temperatures, rarely experienced so late in the year. Even the ever-present wind that held influence over this section of the docks seemed less noticeable. As they started to chat, it might even have been the light-hearted mood that ran through each of them seeming to flourish as they went forwards.

Ultimately, it was none of these things, but rather something much simpler, yet crucial, as they walked only millimetres apart. Indeed, it was as his hand had brushed against hers for an electrifying split second, only for exactly the same thing to occur moments later, that he realised this night was to be unlike any that had come before. She, in turn, knew only that what was to be revealed by the coming night could no longer be circumvented.

And yet, despite his valiant attempts both at levity and to espouse a relaxed attitude, nervousness like never before stalked him. Such a thing betrayed him at every attempt at either speech or simply breathing with short shallow breaths that tightened his chest and his throat. So much so, it was all that he could do to keep his sentences short and to the point and of course to avoid the one thing that he wanted to talk about more than any other.

"Nasty do, that plane going up like that, Miss C, and the four special ops personnel, was it, who were killed? What happened to them?"

She looked straight at him, even though the dark cloaked much of her expression; as usual her eyes betrayed nothing of all that was hidden. "Yes, terrible thing, that. They say it was a fuel leak and the plane just went up before the gangway could be attached. I'm told one of the engines caught fire as they were heading over the Irish Sea. I wonder if the flames in the engine were not fully extinguished and the fire spread. The two pilots managed to get out, barely, by smashing the front screens. I am afraid the occupants were just charred remains by the time the fire was put out. The Americans are not best pleased about losing four of their best men, or a plane worth millions."

"It's a good job it was in the dead of night and well away from the terminal building. I can't see that it was due to the fire spreading, though. If you look at that wing it's largely intact, the fire must have been well out when they came to rest, unlike the fuselage, of which little remains."

"All in all it's a nasty do, though, Tim. I am not sure what Uncle Sam will miss most, that transport plane or the four black-ops forces members who were killed when it went up."

"Do you think it went up in an accident, Miss C, or do you reckon someone set it on fire deliberately, to cover their tracks, perhaps?"

"Whoa, Tim, I'm sure it was just a nasty accident. Did they find anything?"

"That was the thing; they only found spent shell casings from the guns of the four men. Or rather, I should say three revolvers were empty and the other had a full magazine."

She held her breath. They'd had conversations like this before and she recognised one such opening up now.

"Oh, why was that then?"

"Well, don't you see?"

"No."

"He was the first to die!"

She nodded invisibly in the blackness as she turned to him reflexly, in order to offer her open expression as further confirmation of her surprise and naivety as to what might have happened.

"So, maybe they all turned on each other and then took each other out?"

"No, Miss C, I reckon it was a *hit*, an execution." A tiny sliver of moonlight caught his shaking head before being eclipsed.

"Surely not! Who could or would mount such an operation?" she began, then hurried on quickly; being reminded how searching his questions could be. "Well, Tim, I am sure they deserved it. Maybe it was Divine retribution?"

"Perhaps, and yes, I agree, they deserved their fate. But, Miss C, I think this was man-made."

"Very well then, if that's the case, *how* were they killed? Nobody could attack four highly trained Special Forces operatives in a confined space without a weapon; it would be suicide."

"Ah yes, but of course, the person or persons who carried out the hit had *weapons* but just not guns."

"No guns! Surely that's fanciful against special ops personnel. It would be nigh on impossible to take them out without firearms. If one was going to the trouble of a hit why not rely on surprise and open up with machine pistols?"

"That's an easy one, Miss C. They couldn't risk shell casings being found."

"Ah, okay then, so they talked them to death." The depth of the darkness obscured the fleeting smile she sent him in that moment, but her delicate pause had betrayed what was on her face anyway.

"No, no," he said, a bit like a schoolteacher, as he paused and she waited for what she guessed could only be more questions, "I think they used knives."

"Knives!"

"Yes, it's the only way. He or they couldn't risk hand-to-hand combat in a confined space; knives would be perfect. A knife is easy to find once it's over and one could remove it and then, to cover one's tracks, set the plane on fire. Maybe use an untraceable accelerant that would be easily masked, like petrol, do you think? Sprinkle it liberally within the fuselage when all the action's over then get out quickly. By doing so they could ensure that nobody would ever know."

"Indeed, Tim, I'm sure that's what they would hope. But, wait a minute surely using a knife in a confined space with four highly trained opponents would be a very risky operation?"

"Not for a knife specialist; someone with amazing accuracy and who was able to work in tight spaces."

"But, surely, he or she would be gunned down!"

"No, remember the old joke about the space shot to the sun?"

"Yes?"

"Go at night!"

"Oh yes, I see." She would have loved to have laughed but, in that moment, nervousness was firmly in charge and she waited for what she knew must come next. Making one last attempt to throw him off, she continued, "So, we have our knife specialist, but how did he or she see enough to kill four men in total darkness?"

"There was a mobile phone, or I should say, the charred remains of a mobile phone; either this was used to provide illumination, or they had night vision goggles."

"So, let's get this right, a knife specialist, confined space and night vision goggles. Sounds like a heady and improbable mix to me," she offered, in her deepest and most doubtful of tones.

"Yes, that's it. I think you have it, exactly! What's more, I know who has done this."

"You do?" The words that came sounding much more squeaky than their usual rich timbre.

"Yes, Miss Clancy." She shot him a glance, just as a broad shaft of silvery light was released by the moon's being liberated by a cloud sliding by, that took a millisecond longer than usual for her to mask with shock and surprise.

"I think it was Brady; he's an expert with a knife."

"He *is*?" She coughed loudly as if now having to clear her throat. "Yes, I mean, Tim, *he* is," she affirmed as best she could, by using the deepest register that she could persuade her voice to plumb.

"Not that I could ever approach him with that; this is just between us two."

"Well, Tim, he won't hear it from me."

"And to be truthful I don't blame him. I think the Americans were trying to extract them before they could face justice and I'm told HM Government agreed to them being deported. Scot-free, just like that. Shameful, that's what it is!" He snapped his fingers.

"Did they?"

"Well, that's what Griff and Tracy say." It was now his turn to nod reassuringly in her direction.

"Oh well, that must be the case then, Tim."

"Well done, Tim, putting that all together, maybe you are correct."

"I'd want to congratulate him, if I was walking with him now; I'd say it to his face. Maybe there were two, what do you think?"

"No, Tim, you are getting a bit carried away now. Two! Surely not in that confined space."

"No, I'm sure you are right, Miss C, it would have to be someone very slim, willowy, flexible and lithe. Someone who was very fast and strong, yet able to work in close confines." The moonlight revealed him to be looking at her form as he assembled more adjectives.

She shifted uncomfortably, perhaps for a moment, and then came that steady neutral gaze aimed squarely in his direction: one that would mask everything. A second or two later, the dense clouds blotted out light from the moon, saving her from further scrutiny. She knew that only silence would serve at this point.

"Yes, guess you are right, Miss Clancy, perhaps just Brady on his own."

He'd done his best to deflect his own thoughts, and his animated discussion nearly accomplished this. Then, however, their hands brushed tantalisingly together, once again, and just after they had done so, he was reminded of the person who was with him, the person he'd been desperate, for some weeks, to be invited to accompany on one of her walks. Ultimately, his head was bursting with even more excitement and, as always, questions; especially one question that he held as being more urgent than all others, and indeed more important than any question he'd ever asked in his relatively young life, as it surged within. In that moment he sensed that they were still closer, even before their hands made fleeting contact once more. As they did so, he felt a jolt like electricity, but stronger, course through his body.

He knew he could bear it no longer. It was time. And yet, how to pose such a question? The agony and ecstasy of the cusp of indecision held him speechless for that moment as they walked. Moreover, he'd learned so much. He knew that the best strategy, despite his excitement, was to wait until she was ready to speak and to engage in personal things; not about work.

He did his best to calm his breathing. Even as he did so the short shallow breaths seemed to take total control to the point of mocking him. 'Control your breathing and you'll control the situation' was one thing, among many, that she'd taught him. At such time he knew he'd have his chance – perhaps. Or more likely, he'd simply never raise the courage. His moment came sooner than he'd thought and, in so doing, banished all his uncertainty.

"I'm hoping, if you are correct, that it's a fitting end to this mission. I mean for Brady, at least he will have some satisfaction of seeing the guilty get their comeuppance. Although officially it's been put down as a freak accident. So, Tim, may I ask?"

"Hey, Miss Clancy, isn't that my line?"

She laughed; such a laugh was to re-invigorate her light-hearted mood and subsequent events would bring a lifting of the sadness that had stalked her for most of her life. "Not tonight, Tim, I'm going to borrow it just for a moment or two." She began again, her voice reaching its highest register with her carefree mood.

"So, may I ask?"

"Oh, okay then, what would you like to know?" He did his best to appear reluctant but this was the last emotion that held sway upon him. Finally his breathing slowed just a little, the tightness in his chest eased as he wondered just what it was that she was about to ask.

The reflex laugh came again. "Sorry, Tim, I couldn't resist it. I was just going to ask you how you were?"

"Oh, Miss Clancy, I am fine, absolutely fine and I believe it's all down to you. I finally read the transcripts from the time I was shot by Leonid, the Russian assassin."

"Yes, I know Janet told you I just left you there to die. I am so sorry she said that, Tim." Her voice now wavered with nervousness; an unusual emotion for her yet this, too, seemed to be an appropriate accompaniment to their mood that night. Her uncertain look had, for the moment, been eclipsed like the moon behind dark, pregnant clouds.

"Although I don't really remember anything, the doctors say this is not unusual with such cases of trauma and collapse; I read how you swam over there and knifed him before he could shoot us all."

"Yes, Tim, that's just about it." Her nervousness persisted, despite his eagerness to carry their conversation forwards.

"Was there anything else, Miss C?"

"No Tim, I think you just about have most of it."

"Well, Toby says that you did the only thing possible. I agree with him, you had to get over there and silence Leonid. I've seen pictures of that taxi; it's riddled with bullets that passed right through. We'd have *all* been killed, including the medical team, with such a cruel and indiscriminate killer."

"I knew that was what I had to do. He wasn't going to stop shooting until either he'd run out of ammunition or someone had stopped him."

"The only thing I'm a bit vague about is the bit where you ran back. It says in the report that you knelt by my collapsed body, the paramedic gave you his coat, you shouted at the film crew and that is when Janet turned up?"

"Yes, I think you have it all. I don't think there was anything more to add." Despite the limited light, her large brown eyes were now offered in his direction so, once more, he could detect no trace of the events and words she'd chosen to obscure."

"And Janet?"

"To be truthful, she is correct; she is the one who saved you. She bared both her forearms and told the medics that her blood was 'O' negative and they should take it all. That was a brave and selfless thing for her to do, Tim. And it was she who shook the medical team into trying some more. She just wasn't going to take 'no' for an answer. As she would have it, she really kicked some butt!"

"Do you think she just used me to infiltrate Horizon? Was my collapse her 'way in'?"

"Yes, I suppose so, but in fairness to her I think she really cared for you. Unfortunately, I suspect she cared for her assignment and the CIA somewhat more. When she learned of our mission and the secrets that lay behind it, I guess her true colours came to the fore. She is, after all, a professional, regardless of her somewhat full-on methods."

"And full-on they were Miss C. Funny, my Mum hated her the moment she set eyes on her."

"Oh, why was that?" her eyes widened with surprise.

"I suppose, in truth…well, you know."

She nodded for him to continue but just at that point he decided to keep his own counsel, fearing initially that he would only embarrass her and then, having done so, he'd never get the chance to ask the one question that scorched within his brain, like a fulminating liquid that couldn't be held by any vessel. He knew that there was more, so much more, that he wanted to say and, of course, to ask and yet his nerve had failed, just at the crucial point.

"Anyway, she didn't like her, not one bit."

"And was that it, just that she didn't like her?"

"No, not quite." His breathing reverted to a gasping pattern as he tugged hurriedly but shallowly on the night air.

Once again Clancy nodded in the hope that he'd continue but his thoughts had already stalled with his nervousness. He changed the subject while he attempted to summon more courage.

"Then I found out that she was just a plant to spy on us; to spy on all of us. Having infiltrated the organisation, she just waited for the next big mission. She fed everything back to her masters for her own gain and theirs."

"I think the CIA had detected that Horizon was being called upon by the Government more and more to handle tricky problems, below the radar and with no questions asked.

This in turn meant that the Establishment could always claim credit if things went well or deny all knowledge if things went badly – all this without having to summon the more formal security services." Sensing that she was unwittingly moving away from the thing she wanted to emphasise, she corrected this, "Don't forget though, Tim, I think she definitely had feelings for you."

"I am not so sure about that, Miss Clancy, but thank you for that anyway." Despite the dim light she saw that he'd looked away as his words, now like a confession continued, "I feel so stupid in being used in that way. She made me feel as if I was special. I should have known that no girl would be interested in a serious relationship with me. I should have known that the whole thing was just a sham. I feel so embarrassed and so ashamed, to think that taking up with her nearly got us all killed." He'd deliberately drifted into a peripheral part of the truth: for he knew that he could never confess that he'd engaged with the American to attempt to dilute his persistent longing and thoughts for another – one who spoke in that moment.

"Whoa, Tim, I think you are being very hard on yourself. There is certainly nothing to feel shame about!"

"I should have known that no girl is interested in me, *really* interested that is. When they have got to know me, that's when they disappear. I feel such a failure."

She stared at him for some time, using the pause to align her raging thoughts. For once, she was sorry that the dense and fickle clouds obscured her expression, as she would have wanted him to see her face and perhaps some of her feelings that existed in that moment.

"Gosh, Tim, I can't see that, perhaps you've just been unlucky. Maybe you just haven't met the right girl?"

He knew this most definitely to be untrue, but accepted that he could never declare as such. "Hopeless in love *and* unlucky, Miss C."

Once again, she hoped that the non-compliant moon would be available to illuminate the incredulity and some of the other thoughts that were evident on her expression. Surely he must be aware that he was worthy of so many more things than his low self-esteem would permit − and that to her, was, without doubt, everything.

"Oh, well, I am sure that things will change for you, Tim."

He could only hope that this was the case and at that moment the question that burned within tortured him just a little more. Once again he held back from voicing it.

"So, what's happened to her, Miss Clancy?"

"She's been deported back to the US. I can't see her making a return to Blighty any time soon. No doubt she'll be working missions in other areas in which America seeks influence."

"And to think we were hoping to prosecute them. Seems what goes around comes around. If Brady sets eyes on her he's already told her what he'll do to her."

"Yes, I believe you are correct, especially as regards Brady. Anyway, Tim, you were telling me about your Mum?" Once again Clancy had sensed the impasse in his thoughts and brought him back to that point.

"I was?"

"Yes, I believe so."

He tried to smile but it was transformed into something of a grimace as his nerves bested him, once again. Mercifully, he managed to supress it quickly enough for even Clancy not to detect just how much he'd learned from her.

"Yes, she didn't like her because, well really…"

"Yes, well really, what?"

"Well, yes, well really, I suppose because she wasn't you!"

"That's very nice of your mum, Tim," she offered, being pleased with arriving at the answer, as well as with its content.

"I guess you could say she's a big fan of yours."

"And, of course, I am of her." Clancy's eyes flared in the near-darkness.

He stopped, turning suddenly to face her, then thought better of it, only to somehow manage to at least begin the question that he realised could wait no longer.

"Miss Clancy, may I ask?"

"Oh, oh, what is that Tim?"

He breathed in slowly and held his breath for a second before beginning the exhalation which would calm his racing brain and slow the tempest within his heart – a trick which, like so many other things, he'd learned from her. In that nuance of time the vast dark clouds somehow slipped by, liberating the amber-like glow given off by the October moon. More than this, her smile washed over him like sunshine on a summer's day as she recognised the importance of whatever it was he was about to ask. In truth, she knew not only that the moment had arrived when he had to ask it, but also that she owed him an answer – though perhaps not quite yet.

"I wanted to ask. What happened that day in my E-Type?"

"E-type?"

"My E-type, the red one; remember, the day I took you home to have lunch?"

"You did?"

"Yes, you came home with me to meet my Mum and Dad."

"Oh, yes I remember, vaguely. What of it?"

Her face remained completely impassive with perhaps a slight trace of disinterest as she perfectly masked the turmoil within. She wasn't quite ready. Furthermore, she needed to be certain that his enquiry was of significant moment to him and not simply polite chat. She would not have to wait long for clarification.

"Oh, I was wondering if, well… You don't remember, so it couldn't have been important."

He looked away in that moment, being unable to hide the depth of disappointment that ran over his features.

"What was it, Tim, it must have been something for you to ask me about it after all these months? I don't remember anything special, apart from meeting your parents and, of course, your magnificent open-top Jaguar. Was there anything else?"

"No, not really, I suppose, Miss C."

"There must be something, Tim, pass it by me?"

"Oh, not really, it's just that you kissed me."

"I kissed you!"

He could have kicked himself. Could he have imagined the whole thing during the time he was in a coma? Even if it was real, it could have had no special relevance to her if she'd forgotten such a thing, when it was the *only* thing he'd thought about ever since. Evidently it was too great a leap to expect her to remember one of the most important events in his life. He felt so embarrassed and so stunned that he couldn't even think of a way to move the conversation on. Eventually he sought refuge in limited words. Moreover, he'd not quite sensed the resurgence of her light-hearted mood, nor the smile about which his life revolved – as a fertile planet around the sun.

"Oh it's nothing, Miss Clancy..." he offered unhappily, his speech now faltering like a car stalling on a steep slope.

"Well, I wonder, what was it like? Was it like this?" She gave him a quick peck on the cheek.

"No, yes, well, I suppose that's all it must have been," he lied to save himself, and her, from further embarrassment.

"Very well then, was it like this?"

Suddenly she stopped walking, turning to him in one smooth movement; she held his left arm, ever so gently at first, but then with a grip which signified that something of much greater moment was now in progress. She gently turned his torso to face her. He waited, not daring to breathe.

Within a second her palms had been placed lightly, but momentously, either side of his neck. Her lush and sparkling lips were around his in the time it took his stampeding heart to form one beat. As he felt his unrestrained heart reach even greater heights; dizziness, to the point of fainting, nearly came to claim him, although he knew that this was one moment that he could neither miss, nor wish to ever end.

"Yes, it was a bit like that."

"A bit like that? Very well, then, how about this?"

Her lips were around his once again. Despite the poor light, he knew those gorgeous eyes were upon him too, her gaze coursing through him like water giving life to an arid desert.

Her smooth hands held him while her long fingers were passed, as they had that day, up the back of his neck and on through his thick and wavy hair. His lips now tingled and he felt even more light-headed than before.

"You know, Miss Clancy, that was close but I think it was more like this." Strong arms slipped around her slim waist while he held her with a force that conveyed a passion that he'd waited all his life to convey – and finally been given the chance to reveal. He kissed her as if it was, at the same time, the last thing he would ever do in his life and yet be the first of millions that would follow. Vitality flowed through them like a bolt of lightning discharged by a developing electric storm to the earth that had been waiting hungrily to receive it. She could barely breathe; it was her turn now to feel dizzy as the feelings running through him finally found vent within her.

After an age he released her, ever so slowly, his gentle movement standing stark against the passion that had been unleashed.

"Ah, yes, Tim, I remember now. Wow! Yes, that must have been it. How could I have forgotten?"

He laughed. "It was a bit like that, Miss Clancy."

"Tim, it won't do"

"It won't?" He looked dispirited again.

"No, Tim, It won't do, you calling me Miss Clancy. I do have *another* name you know?"

"I am told so, Miss Clancy."

"Well, if we are to be friends, and good friends, then it's high time you started using it."

"I am not sure I can. I think it will need time."

"Oh well, perhaps with a bit of regular practice?"

"Could still take a while, though, Miss C."

"I'll be patient, don't worry"

"I promised you that I'd tell you the day I pulled you out of that casino"

As the scales fell from his eyes, he realised that he now knew exactly what had happened in the casino and, even more crucially, also what happened when Clancy had come back for him as he lay dying on the roadside.

He laughed. "It was you! All along it was you, how could I not have seen that? You came for me to pull me out of that casino. It wasn't Toby! You asked him to let you run that mission. I remember. I remember it all! Thank you, thank you, Penny."

"Ah well Tim, in that case just one thing to be said. I think it's time for the two of us to go off and do something, just we two?"

"Oh no, Penny, I have given up playing cards, I told you."

"Who's interested in cards?"

Her hands gripped his and she gently turned him back the way they'd come; their pace now picking up for reasons that they both understood.

The darkest depth of the night would find them entwined in each other's arms. Here she was, the most beautiful girl he'd ever seen, the one he admired and respected more than any other. The one he'd been in love with since the day she first came for him. Furthermore, he now knew that he was the person she'd come back for. She who'd told him things, wonderful things, even as he lay dying, or so she'd been told, in her arms. Now they were alone at last. Strong arms held her as the soft duvet enveloped them both.

He gently whispered her name, as if he'd been rehearsing doing so since the first day they met. He repeated it, having quietly postponed and stored all those occasions when he'd wanted to voice that name. The one that had surged through him since the day he'd discovered it. He caressed her soft, lustrous hair and held her lithe form close as he did so.

As the passion built for each of them, suddenly she started trembling and began to sob. Despite the total darkness, he gently wiped away the tears with a careful sweep from his hand. He then, slowly and tantalisingly, kissed each cheek now swollen and sore.

"I'm frightened, Tim. I'm not sure I can do this. Please don't hurt me."

Her sobs were both hard for her to contain and for him to receive.

"I'll never ever hurt you, it's my promise. You don't have to do this, *we* don't have to do this, not now, not ever. And as for being scared, then me too, Penny. I love you and there is no hurry. We can take as long as we need. I'm with you now and I am hoping this will be not just for now but forever, so we can take all the time that we need. I have so many strong feelings for you and there are many more ways for me to demonstrate them, and I'll spend the rest of my life in finding every single one. I know I'll love you forever at the very least, we'll look forwards to a bright future not back to the dark days of the past; and I promise to be with you every step of the way. So, how about a nice cup of tea and a game of cards?"

She laughed as images presented in her mind. He went on, desperately trying to make her tears and her distress sublimate in the darkness.

"I knew it was you, that very first smile and I knew there and then, ever since the day that *you* asked Toby to let you run that mission. How glad I am that you did, that you came for me and re-booted my life, that had been a dry and empty shell, and gave it purpose. I ask for no more than to be with you in whatever way you feel at ease with." He kissed her again and again. He gently stroked her cheek and caressed the long fragrant hair. "So, cards anyone?"

Suddenly, her crying stopped, but not the trembling. She knelt on the bed and framed his face in her hands. Despite the darkness he could sense that she was staring intensely at him.

The trembling seemed to become more marked. As she held him firmly her words began.

"If we do this...."

"If we do this, Tim…." She gripped him now almost to the point of pain. He'd guessed that something above and beyond being catastrophically orphaned had happened to her. He now understood so much more and knew that what she'd experienced could only be truly dreadful. As she spoke her voice carried more urgency.

"I told you, Penny we *don't* have to do this; not now, not ever, if that's not what you want."

"Tim, do you mind, could we?"

"Yes, of course, what exactly?"

She laughed now, having been distracted from the cruellest of thoughts.

"Do you mind if we have the light on?"

"No, of course not. Do you want just the bedside or all of them?"

"All of them, please."

This was it, the first of the many secrets she would share over the coming years. Even so he hadn't quite guessed that this had been her torment. Deep in the night, when absolute black reigned, was when Roy had come to her and done such horrible things while she wept uncontrollably, as he held his hand over her mouth with some force to prevent the sound of sheer torment from escaping. Now had come the light and, as it flooded the room, it banished that suffering and those dark deeds. Most vitally, she knew this was the way they'd proceed, as friends, as confidants and as lovers − but always in the light.

Her svelte, toned body relaxed; she kissed him repeatedly, as their bodies became closer still. Passion was re-kindled; she knew that at last she'd found someone who understood, who wanted her for herself and not for any other criteria. She was ready. Moreover, she knew that she was with the only person who could have made all this possible. This was something she'd known the day that she met him.

"Cards was not what I had in mind, Tim. Don't you dare, come here!"

"No cards, then, Miss Clancy?"

She laughed, "What happened to Penny?"

"Oh yes, she's the girl; the one I loved the day she came for me and whisked me out of that casino and into her car. I've been begging her to tell me her name ever since."

"That's the one!"

"Oh well, Penny, if you insist."

Their bodies folded as one. For the first time but, as it would come to pass, far from the last time in her life she experienced feelings, borne out of an act that represented love rather than lust, and sharing of that love, not an abuse – an act that was gentle, selfless and attuned to her needs, not someone else's.

She thought, fleetingly, about that person who represented an abomination and the corruption of an act of love and tenderness, instead visiting upon her pain and torment rather than pleasure. Although she realised that such thoughts would intrude again, she'd now found a pathway, and a person to lead her, from such cruel, desolate memories associated with the dark and not the light. As the pure and gentle love worked its magic on her body she relaxed more, thus heightening her experience and enjoyment, with surely the only person she could have responded to, and this would be, after so many years of torture, the relationship she deserved.

After the climax had come for each of them, she held him and ran her fingers through the blond, thick, slightly wavy hair as she kissed him again. He whispered her name, "Penny, thank you for pulling me from that casino."

"Tim, I think you saved me, too. I knew it was you during all those days I spent watching your unhappy life, I just knew you were the one."

She wondered later if it was her mention of an unhappy life that triggered her thoughts at that juncture. She sat up and stared through the window towards the first light of dawn. She held the duvet up to her chin against the cold that up to that point she hadn't really felt. He sat up too but, although not sensing the detail of her thoughts, he knew that speech at this time was unwanted. She stared into the middle distance now past him, wondering how life would have turned out for her if, on that fateful day, those points had not failed and she still had her family. She remained immersed in her own thoughts for so long as he studied, not for the first time, every aspect and curve of her pretty face. A lonely tear made a slow journey from the corner of one of her eyes. He sensed the sadness that was engraved on a face normally covered by a mask: a mask that had just slipped as she watched the dawn announce a new day.

Eventually, he just had to ask, "Penny, may I ask?"

"Oh, oh, Tim, what would you like to know?"

"Well, Penny, can I ask, why me? Why me, when you could have any man you want?"

"Very well, Tim, of all the questions you've posed, this is the easiest to answer!"

She smiled; the kiss she gave him was the gentlest he'd ever experienced, for it existed fleetingly on his cheek like a butterfly with much to do on a summer's day. Suddenly, it was gone and yet memories of that touch would be with him forever.

More than this, the look she offered conveyed far more than any words, and suddenly he understood. Also revealed to him in that moment were some of the thoughts that lay behind those pretty eyes, fixed upon him; eyes the colour of spun caramel. Eyes that could obscure, when she chose, but also reveal in equal part. All at once, he understood and he knew what now lay between them was not only precious but, also, likely to last forever.

She thought, but only for a moment, as she went back to revisit that excited teenager sitting facing her parents at the start of a railway journey, how delighted they'd be for her.

Then, she flopped back on the pillow; raised one slender arm towards the ceiling while the other came up to frame her lush lips as she gave off a cry of delight. For a discovery came over her that very moment as she cried, as she wept and as she laughed with the ecstasy of discovering something that her sad, cruel life and her long, lonely journey had promised was waiting for her − somewhere. It was, for her, without doubt, the final truth. Clancy had found love.

THE END

www.ingramcontent.com/pod-product-compliance
Lightning Source LLC
Chambersburg PA
CBHW061153170626
46809CB00003B/1082